WICKEI

MW00908340

Madison Sevier

Erotic Romance

Secret Cravings Publishing
www.secretcravingspublishing.com

A Secret Cravings Publishing Book

Erotic Romance

Wicked by Nature
Copyright © 2013 Madison Sevier
Print ISBN: 978-1-63105-155-5

First E-book Publication: December 2013
First Print Publication: April 2014

Cover design by Dawné Dominique
Edited by E. L. Felder
Proofread by Amanda Ward
All cover art and logo copyright © 2013 by Secret Cravings
Publishing

PUBLISHER
Secret Cravings Publishing
www.secretcravingspublishing.com

Dedication

This book is dedicated to my past. You threw everything you could at me, changed the truth to fit your own selfish desires, but you didn't win. You pushed me to the edge of my sanity by taking the very thing that meant the world to me. I fell but I got back up over and over again. You attempted to turn me into the evil person you wanted everyone to believe me to be, but I proved you wrong.

In the end, I realized I didn't have to be wicked to fight you. I only needed to have the one thing you could never take away from me. It took so long for me to realize what it was and in a shockingly obvious, very public, moment of clarity in an historic place, I found it. I discovered there was something you still hadn't succeeded in destroying. The one thing that had been hidden beneath the pain, the anger, the guilt and the one thing that had kept me going even when I believed I could go no further. Hope. It was there all along and it always will be. Thank you for showing me what I truly needed and who I truly am. Bless your heart.

WICKED BY NATURE
Madison Sevier
Copyright © 2013

Prologue

There were so many signs along the way. Not just little, insignificant things. No. There were giant, red, warning signs that should've crossed my line of vision at least once. Then again, I'm sure they did. Perhaps if I had paid more attention, things would've been different. I ignored every one of them and saw only what I wanted to see. My negligence almost cost me my life and the lives of those around me, all because I fell in love with a demon. In fact, I'm glad I fell in love with him. I know you must think I'm a nut-job, but if I hadn't met Shawn Richardson, my life would still be a lie.

I lived the lie for so long that I became that lie. If I hadn't stopped practicing magic, maybe I would've seen what was coming. The list of ifs and maybes could go on forever. The fact is, I still couldn't have stopped any of the events that unfolded. They were meant to happen. Each of them was planned long before I was even born. Call it predetermined or predestined, either way, knowing ahead of time wouldn't have mattered.

The day I, Selena Barnes, found out the truth started out like any other day. I had a huge list of pre-wedding duties and errands to complete and I was behind as usual. Maybe the fact that I could never seem to get it together, could never complete any of those tasks should have been a sign in itself? Maybe it was. There I go again with the 'maybe'. See? It's an endless, pointless circle of questioning.

When I met Shawn, I already knew I was a witch, a good witch. And from our very first conversation, I knew Shawn was anti-paranormal. He hated anyone and anything associated with it. When the subject came up, I lied. I told him of my parents, but I never explained that I, too was a paranormal creature. To be honest, he was a man to fulfill my needs, nothing more, and I didn't think that extra bit of information would help me get what I wanted. I simply never mentioned that I was a witch and that night, I never gave thought to any consequences from our conversation, or lack thereof. I honestly never imagined my lie would need to hold up as long as it did. I hadn't thought past our first night together, and in a small town, it isn't easy to get away with any act, seen or unseen, let alone pretending to be something you aren't. Why did I allow the charade to continue for so long? Because, by the time I realized we were in love, it was too late. I'd learned to live without my powers. They no longer mattered to me. Shawn believed in me, he loved me and he became my world. Or so he claimed.

Even when the 'townies' told him multiple times that I was a witch and I would one day come to my senses and destroy him for the terrible things he had done, Shawn dismissed their claims. He told me over and over that he loved me.

"No amount of gossip will change that, Selena. Besides, wouldn't I know if you were a witch? Come on, I won't allow those harpies to destroy our relationship." He claimed to know me better than anyone else did and I believed every word he said.

Shawn Richardson is a powerful man and could've lived anywhere. Once, I had a fleeting moment when I wondered why a man such as he would ever move to a town like Salem Ridge. If I was someone with his beliefs, I would never live in a place built as a haven for the paranormal. But at the time, who was I to judge him? As I did with every other concern or suspicion I had about Shawn, I pushed it to the back of my mind and only later, much later, would all of those tiny pieces of information come back with such alarming impact that they could no longer be ignored.

Shawn owned the largest factory as well as many homes and small businesses in Salem Ridge, Indiana. If anyone crossed him, he would fire them or evict them. Maybe I was not only subconsciously afraid of him leaving me, but also afraid of him, the man everyone claimed he truly was. Business was business and business was his life. I knew that when I met him and I was grateful that he wasn't a 'clingy' man. Rumors and allegations of Shawn being a philanderer and a demon ran rampant. I spent many nights crying, questioning Shawn and myself about who or what he really was. Of course, Shawn allayed those fears and insecurities with lavish presents and sweet words that dripped from his sugar-coated tongue. And since I'd sworn off using my powers, I soon began to believe the gossipers were nothing more than hateful, vindictive mudslingers and I convinced myself they were wrong.

I would've been able to sense if something was evil or otherworldly about the man I loved, wouldn't I? I'd never been very self-assured and with Shawn, I could remain naïve and sheltered. Or so I thought. Ignoring my gut instinct had always been one of my major character flaws. Somehow, after all of my mother's teachings, I'd forgotten that not listening to your inner voice could also prove deadly.

After my parents died in a horrible accident, from a spell gone wrong, I couldn't bear to be reminded of the very thing that had taken my mother and father from me. I packed away my beloved altar items and my antique crystal pendulum was hidden for safe keeping. I couldn't stand the thought of destroying those items, those pieces of myself. Maybe even then I knew I would one day need them again.

The day after my parents were buried, Shawn proposed and it caused an uproar as soon as the townies realized I'd truly never practice magic again, not with him in my life. I had 'pissed my heritage away' according to them. In their eyes, practicing our Craft was a necessity, as essential as breathing, so I became known as a traitor. Breaking Shawn and I apart became their one, their only, goal. By doing so, they must've thought they could bring me 'back to their side'. I stopped going into town on a regular basis just so I could avoid any uncomfortable situations or confrontations, so I wouldn't have to hear what I believed to be lies about the man I loved.

How could I have known they were telling the truth about Shawn? Maybe because I knew they'd tried to tell him the truth about me? But that little clue was invisible to me. How could I have known what a monster Shawn was and that he was viciously lording it over the town, taking whatever he wanted from whomever he wanted?

Without embracing my powers, I was completely blind to his wrongdoings. I was unable, or unwilling, to see why the entire town hated and feared the man I loved. Hell, I didn't even listen to my own familiar, Sterling, and he could be counted on to know everything. Just ask him, he will tell you. He may be just a cat to humans, but for me, he has always been my better half and he definitely knows the truth. He's an integral part of it. Out of everyone, my deceased parents excluded, Sterling is the one being I should've listened to.

Yes, he talks. Most familiars do, but their own witch and other paranormal creatures are the only people with the ability to hear and understand them. And though Sterling is Salem Ridge's equivalent to a 'town crier', I dismissed his repeated verbal attacks against Shawn as nothing more than a territorial pissing contest over me between the two males I loved. Yeah, I had set myself up for one rude awakening. Boy, was it ever.

Where was I? Ah, yes, the day I learned the truth. Or rather, the day I accepted the truth and that epiphany carried so much power that it almost destroyed me and everything around me. To be honest, that was the plan. There were forces at work that wanted nothing more than to end my existence. The following is my account of what led me to finally see that I truly am wicked by nature and I wouldn't change a thing.

Chapter One

"I swear the universe has it in for me! The one day it's a hundred degrees out, I have to end up stuck behind a tobacco farmer hauling a load of dried crop and a school bus that stops at every other house. You've gotta be kidding me! I have so many things to do!" I couldn't pass them without catapulting myself off the side of the mountain, so I was stuck.

"Come on!" Of course, driving a car with broken window cranks and without air-conditioning in the middle of May in southern Indiana wasn't the smartest thing to do. I knew throwing a tantrum wouldn't help, but it was so damn hot!

"Sometimes I wish…almost wish we weren't getting married." I sighed, knowing I didn't mean it, not really.

I had to be the only witch, make that the only woman, in all of Salem Ridge with such horrible luck and lack of common sense. There were times, I really regretted surrendering my powers and on days like this one, sweltering in my much-repaired Beetle, it irked me to no end. I could've whipped up a shiny, new vehicle with a flick of my wrist. But no, I had to take the 'righteous' path.

"Where's that gotten me? On Highway 58 in a compact trash bucket with a motor, that's where."

I sank into my seat and leaned my head back on the headrest. If it hadn't been so freaking hot, I would've cried. But every ounce of water left in my body was pouring out of me in the form of sweat and I couldn't spare a drop for self-pity.

Along with being late for almost everything, I had a tendency to be a bit high-strung and snarky on occasion. I've also been known to bitch and complain to no one in particular, a lot. After spending so much of my free time with only my talking familiar, my cat Sterling, for company, I had morphed into a twenty-five year old scatterbrained, crazy cat lady.

All of that would soon change.

That was the reason for my under-the-gun trip to town, another wedding errand. In two weeks, I'd share my life with

Shawn. I should've been beaming with happiness. Instead, I found myself nervous and on edge quite often. Half of the time I was excited, the other half I felt like I was walking the Green Mile.

"I don't need this. If I don't get to Janice's shop on time, the woman will most certainly explode in a puff of pink satin and taffeta." I huffed.

Janice Sutterfeld was seriously obsessive-compulsive about two things; appointments and the color pink. I already knew she disliked me and being late to pick up my dress would definitely not help the situation. Add in the fact that she adored the one color I absolutely hated, and you'll understand the dread I felt every time I had to visit her boutique. When we were around each other, one could feel the electricity in the air. It was only a matter of time before one of us sparked off.

"Why did I ever order my gown from her?" I grumbled.

In fact, I knew why I chose her as my bridal consultant, but this was one of those 'bitch-to-myself-about-everything' moments so why stop? It wasn't like she was the only bridal boutique in the world, but the next closest one was twenty miles away. And I didn't trust my lemon-bomb of a car to make it there and back for the various fittings and alterations. Besides, I liked the fact that Janice's shop specialized in serving human and paranormal clientele. I assumed she would also treat paranormal clients better than most run-of-the-mill shops.

From what I'd heard around town, Janice did treat other paranormal clients with respect. It was me she had a problem with. Why? Because like everyone else, Janice feels as though I am a traitor to our way of life. Though she and my parents had been friends forever, I knew Janice looked down upon me and tolerated me only out of the respect she still holds for my dearly departed mother and father.

Thank the Goddess this would be my last visit to her shop. At least one detail on my mountainous list of wedding duties would be finished. Don't get me wrong, I was in love with Shawn, but lately the wedding felt more like a one-sided business merger that I needed to close. I'd planned and executed every detail by myself, right down to the color of boxers he would wear. All of my friends had long ago drifted away and Shawn was no help whatsoever. It was beginning to feel like this wedding was more for my benefit than a life-changing event for both of us.

After the agonizingly slow trip through the countryside, the traffic let up just in time for me to obey the twenty-five mile an hour law through town. To be honest, by that point, going twenty-five miles an hour felt like breaking the sound barrier. I was almost sure I'd make it just in time for my appointment and then I'd be home in time for dinner. I sent up a silent prayer, for all I wanted was to get into town, pick up my dress and get back out without any drama or grief.

I parked my sauna-on-wheels in the lot at "Always the Bride". Full of dread and urgency, I jumped out of the car and plowed through the front door. In a blur of blonde hair and flip-flops, I knocked Janice on her perfectly coiffed, pink-clad behind, eliciting from her a sound much like that of a cow giving birth. How was I to know she would be standing right on the other side of the door tapping her Manolos, unsuspecting that I would arrive on the scene with such flamboyancy? Of course that's where she would be. What was I thinking?

"As always, you have perfect timing, Miss Barnes," she snarked as I struggled to push myself off of her pudgy form and onto my own two feet. When she spoke to me, it didn't matter what she said, she always sounded like a very pissed-off snake, with explicit emphasis on her s's. My name slithered out of her mouth, "Mizz Barnzz", and I could've sworn I broke out in hives the moment she looked at me. Why couldn't that woman be civil to me? Trust me, I reciprocated the hostile feeling more and more every time I had to see the viper lady, but I knew I needed to maintain a bit of decorum. After all, today was going to test every bit of self-control I possessed.

"I'm so very sorry, Janice. Here, let me help you."

"No! I mean, no. I'm fine." She jerked away from my outstretched hand and grabbed onto a calamine pink velvet chair, using it to pull herself up off of the floor. Making an elaborate display of dusting off her perfectly pink A-line skirt, her eyes, full of contempt, met mine. I swear if the woman was on fire, she wouldn't let me douse the flames even if I had the only hose and water well in town.

"I really am sorry. I was trying so hard to be on time..."

"No worries," she cut me off, "let's just get your dress tried on so you can leave as quickly as you came in. I do have other clients who show up on time, Selena. I've wasted enough of their time and mine by waiting for you…again."

"Nice to see you, too," I quipped.

The other customers, women who'd been otherwise occupied with the hunt for their own 'perfect' gown, now gave us their undivided attention as they stared at Janice and me, their eyes full of glee. I could almost see them salivating as they visualized who they'd be rushing off to inform first. I'm sure the entire recap of how I knocked Janice down and how in turn, Janice 'dressed me down' would be changed, with more interesting details added for pizazz. The whole town would know within minutes that Janice 'had put that treacherous Selena in her place'.

Just as I'd predicted to myself, within seconds, cell-phones were extracted from some of the younger women's designer bags, while the older ladies—and I use that term loosely—rushed out the door, off to fulfill the gossip quotas for their daily agendas. Another nail in my proverbial social coffin, thanks to my ever present grace and the Viper Lady.

"Lovely", I mumbled.

I knew the few stragglers would not be leaving anytime soon and I'd be fucked and feathered before I gave any of them more mud to sling. Janice clip-clopped away and I averted my gaze, mimicking Janice under my breath as I showed my embarrassed and irritated self into one of the salmon-hued fitting rooms. I closed the door as fast as I could, virtually cutting myself off from the barracuda-like women out front.

"And she bitches about how late *I* was." Twenty minutes later, I still stood there tapping my foot, shivering in my panties and bra. Janice took her sweet-ole time bringing my dress in to me. Evidently, she had no problem leaving me there half-naked and waiting forever! Okay, maybe forever was an exaggeration, but you get my point.

"I should've picked up the dress, said 'screw the fitting' and left." I huffed and counted to ten for the one-hundredth time just as she blew in, looking like an oversized stick of cotton candy.

Her hair, as usual, was a shade of pink and slightly lighter than the azalea color of her clothing and was sprayed within an inch of its life. It was piled high atop her head and bound to outlast any category three storm. Frankly, I'm surprised she hadn't bumped her 'up-do' on the top of the door frame. I suspected the woman owned stock in a major hairspray company. If I ever learned differently, I would have fallen over from shock.

"Here you go, though I'm not sure why a witch with your *abilities* couldn't just whip up the perfect dress. Oh wait, that's right, you're no longer a witch. Silly me." Her smile dripped with venom and Janice held the dress just out of my reach. "It must be nice to simply 'stop' being what you are and carry on with your life as if your past never existed."

I cringed before saying, "Thank you, Janice. Now if you'll excuse me, I believe I can get my gown on without your assistance. Besides, I'm sure you have other things to do." I stepped forward and snatched the dress from her meaty paws.

I was so sick of the constant jabs and comments about my life choices. It was my life! Wasn't that the point of living in a free country? My right to choose who and what I wanted or didn't want to be shouldn't have caused so much controversy. Why were these people so intent on destroying our lives? I couldn't stop the movie-like images of the past few years that washed over my mind as I stood there under Janice's scrutiny.

When the townspeople failed to turn Shawn against me, they switched their attention to his actions. At least two or three times a month for the past four years of dating, Janice and her friends had brought stories of Shawn's philandering and demonic escapades to my attention. Yes, they tried to convince me Shawn was a demon! Can you believe that? Small towns, you gotta love 'em'. None of that made our relationship flow smoothly. We'd had so many bumps along the way, and we'd broken up and gotten back together countless times.

I finally learned to ignore them as best as I could. I figured if they were focused on Shawn, they were at least leaving some other poor soul alone. Don't get me wrong, their constant attempts to break Shawn and I up, were becoming monotonous and harrowing, but I knew in my heart they were lying mudslingers.

Shawn was an affluent member of the county and owned businesses left and right. In fact, he owned businesses belonging to the biggest of the gossipers. These people never said a word to

Shawn's face. Instead, ninety-five percent of the time I was on the receiving end of their verbal brutality.

I learned long ago to not bother Shawn with their incessant, ridiculous claims. After bringing one particularly vivid lie to his attention, he became so enraged that he went to the storyteller's home and immediately informed her she was to vacate the premises. Madelyn Jones lost her home and business in record time. Shawn called it "teaching the busy-body a lesson", but the townspeople only became more angry. A few months later, Madelyn left town and no one ever saw her again. Many believed she went to live with her daughter in Maine. Other people had their own theory of her departure and none of them included a happy ending.

"Ahem! I do hope you're pleased with the alterations this time. You're the only customer, paranormal or human, who has ever demanded so many fittings." Once again, Janice was terse and only too happy to point out my faults whenever I came to the shop.

"I'm sure it will be fine this time, Janice," I said, doing my best to ignore her latest snide remark as she attempted to grab the gown from me, intent on assisting me in trying on the endless yards of silk and lace. Both of us stood there, our hands holding the dress tightly from opposite sides. One wrong move and it would have ripped down the middle.

"You know this dress is a one of a kind creation. It deserves to be showcased in an elaborate wedding, not in some generic courthouse ceremony. I wish it was getting the attention it demands," she mused, never releasing her grip.

"Well, for your information we are not getting married at the courthouse." I tugged slightly.

"Oh that's right. I heard Judge Weston won't allow you to have your wedding there." Janice tugged back. "After all, not many people approve of your union and with the election coming up it would look bad for Judge Weston if he was to perform your ceremony. What would happen to the poor old man if he wasn't re-elected? Can you imagine the devastation that would befall his family, all because of you? The old man might actually end up divorced. His wife would leave. Sylvia could never handle being with a failure." The slit of a smile she wore reeked of false sincerity as she stepped nose-to-nose with me, my dress still in our grasp.

She made it sound as though she was concerned for Judge Weston's well-being, but nothing could be farther from the truth. Janice only cared about what was best for Janice and she didn't fool me. There had to be something of benefit to Janice if Judge Weston got re-elected. My gut told me she was more than likely sleeping with the sweet old man.

Maybe that's why Janice was being so persnickety with me? She must think I knew her little secret. You'd think Janice would be nicer if that were the case. The suspicious side of me became flooded with the itch to throw out a truth spell and get to the bottom of Janice's behavior. No! I couldn't. I swore I wouldn't tap into my abilities for any reason and I meant to keep it that way. Even if curiosity killed me, I wouldn't give in to the witchy itch I felt.

Janice was baiting me with her quips and catty comments. And I couldn't help but wonder if she wanted me to zap her with a spell? Could that be it? Was she trying to get me to fall off the witchcraft wagon I had created for myself? Somehow, it incensed me even more to think she would stoop so low. No, I didn't have hundreds of guests coming to the wedding. No, I couldn't just whip up my dream dress. So what? Why couldn't Janice just be happy about making a sale?

"Careful Janice, your bitch is showing," I snarked. Let's face it, the client is always right. Even if the woman loathed me, she had no right to be snippy and unprofessional. I wasn't going to keep playing this game.

"Kindly let go of my dress. This fitting has already taken up too much of your 'precious time' and you are getting hand-sweat all over my silk." She glared at me before begrudgingly releasing her hold on my gown. When she finally stepped away from me, I slid myself into what I considered the perfect wedding dress.

I turned in slow circles, admiring the gorgeous mermaid-style fit and confirmed it to be free of paw stains. During the initial wedding planning stages, I had wanted to order a goddess-like satin sheath, but being in a bridal boutique changed my mind. Although I was surrounded by the many racks of fabulous dresses in every style, I still couldn't find "the one". Instead, I'd asked

Janice for help designing my own gown. She was very cordial and helpful when I handed cash to her, but that soon ended. At first, it didn't bother me. However, after months of the ridiculous tug-of-war between us, my ability to keep a cool head was beyond dwindling.

I tried my best to enjoy the moment, to enjoy the beautiful creation I was wearing. My dress was covered in crystals from bodice to bustle. With the intricate lacework it was truly magnificent and a part of me wished more people would see me in it. A sharp pang of loneliness shot through my stomach when I remembered how much my mother had dreamed of helping me find a wedding dress and how my father would not be there to walk me down the aisle. Tears threatened to spill over as I stood there, truly alone. Sure, Janice was hovering nearby, but she matched and faded into the background.

With my hair unstyled and wearing not one speck of make-up on my face, I had never looked so beautiful and had never felt so lonely. Standing there in the shrine to pink bismuth, my future as Mrs. Shawn Richardson should've finally felt real. I should've glowed with inner joy knowing that in a few short weeks, my fiancé would be home from his overseas business trip and we would be married. We would stand before a non-denominational minister, surrounded by Shawn's business acquaintances and friends as they looked upon us with smiles plastered to their faces. But, there would be no one, not one person, there to support me.

"It's perfect Janice, truly perfect." I cleared my throat and shook off the bout of self-pity.

"Yes, well as much as I would love to congratulate you, I believe you already know how I feel. Now please step out of the gown before you trip and ruin it or something," she hissed. Janice grabbed the zipper, assuring I wouldn't spin around and slap her.

Janice had to know how much this moment meant to me. Every woman dreams of sharing this moment with their mother. Was a little bit of compassion too much to ask? I'd paid seven thousand dollars for this perfect gown and you'd think it would have also bought Janice's kindness! I swear, I wanted to walk out of that salon and march down Main Street doing the cha-cha while wearing it, just to see the look on Janice's face. Of course, the mature side of me won and I remained inside the boutique.

"You're right. I wouldn't want to come back *here* for anything." I innocently batted my eyes and stepped out of my beautiful gown as carefully as I could.

"Finally, something we agree on. I'll get the dress into its bag and you can be on your way." She spun on her heels and exited the room as if I was on fire.

I put my street clothes back on and walked to the front of the store to wait for Miss Congeniality. She practically threw the hideous, mauve garment bag into my arms. Not trusting her, I unzipped the ugly prison to be sure it was my dress. How many shades of pink were there in the world? I wanted to vomit and I silently thanked the Goddess above that I hadn't chosen any shade, light or dark that even resembled anything close to bubble gum, cotton candy or taffy as one of our wedding colors. I'd had enough of that nauseating color to last me a lifetime and if I had to see it again anytime soon, I would explode. As soon as I got home, I'd burn that damn dress bag just for spite!

"Too bad your parents can't be there to see you marry this... *'man'*. I'm sure they'd have a few words to say about all of your recent life-choices. Yes, they would be beaming with pride, wouldn't they?" She smirked.

Now she chose to mention my parents? Now? Why was I even surprised? Did I think I'd get out of the shop before she'd stuck in another dagger?

I reined in my temper before I sent out a hex. Janice had officially pushed every one of my buttons during this visit. I needed to get out of that store before I got myself into serious trouble. Along with refraining from magic for four years, I also hadn't grounded myself nor performed a spiritual cleansing ritual and that wasn't a smart thing to do.

Getting in touch with your inner goddess through meditation was an essential part of the craft. Freeing oneself from the toxicity and stresses of the everyday world helped ensure a healthy, well-balanced spirit. Not to mention, it prevented a witch from 'going off the deep end' and causing unnecessary havoc or harm when she used her magic. And I'd even neglected that one simple ritual.

In other words, I was a powder keg and presently Janice was my match. If I was to open the door to my magic, bad shit would happen and there would be hell to pay for anyone it touched. The

Council of Elders, the most elite and proficient trusted members of paranormal society, would immediately feel whatever power I tapped into. In turn, I would be brought up on serious charges and forced to pay the price for acting out. If that happened, Shawn would find out about my many deceptions and my dreams of a perfect, normal life would be over.

I inhaled what seemed like my hundredth deep breath in the past hour, I said, "So true, Janice, but maybe you can wear a dress like mine for your…what is it, sixth or seventh, wedding? I'm sure it's difficult trying not to repeat your style after so many marriages. What's that saying, 'always the bride', right? Now, have a great day and don't worry one bit about those wrinkles. Some men find them to be very handsome on a woman of your stature and age. Tootles," I winked and sashayed out the door like a super-model wearing my well-worn jeans, tank top and flip-flops. I felt much better when I pictured Janice standing there with her mouth wide open in a perfect 'o' shape as she caught perfect, pink flies with her venomous pie-hole.

I chuckled as I unlocked my car and stepped back, holding the door open for a minute to allow the pent-up heat inside to escape. After placing the gown on the tiny backseat, I climbed in to leave. After only a few moments in my car, I was sweating again. The humidity was relentless! As I slowly pulled out of the parking spot, I wiped sweat from my eye just as another bride-to-be blew her horn, eager to grab the space, and she offered me a one finger salute.

"Wow, what a lady! Her soon-to-be-husband must be so proud." I mused and shook my head. Once out of the parking lot, I pointed my car east which would take me through the town square.

Driving down Main Street, I waved at many of the store owners and townsfolk, hoping my good mood would overpower their animosity towards me. Most of them turned their heads or worse, they looked right through me.

"I wish they'd just get over it already. I can't be the only witch ever to have given up her powers. Jeez!"

I needed to face facts. It didn't matter how many times I explained why I stopped practicing magic, they would never approve of my decision.

"All of these people can go to Hell, every last one of them! Soon I will be married to the man of my dreams. Who needs these small-minded morons and their small-town bullshit, anyway? Shawn is all I'll ever need." I knew I was trying to convince myself things would be okay, but part of me wanted to break down crying. I knew I'd always wonder if things would have been different if I had never met Shawn that night.

Chapter Two

When I met Shawn, I'd only planned on a one-night stand with him. At twenty-one years old, I was simply a young woman looking for a good time and far from ready to settle down in a long-term relationship. My real date had stood me up that night, so I sat at the bar alone attempting to drown my own misery with loud music and a few drinks. When Shawn, tall, dark and handsome, walked into Tooth & Nail, he became a trophy I needed to win even if it was only to soothe my anger with some hot animalistic sex.

His eyes locked with mine and he ambled over to my table.

"May I?"

"Suit yourself."

He summoned the waitress and ordered a round of drinks. "Beer for the lady and I'll have your finest scotch on the rocks."

"Scotch, huh?"

"Only the best. I'm a man of impeccable taste. Must be why I spotted you. I've always been drawn to incredible things and people. The name's Shawn Richardson, you might've heard of me. I practically own this town."

"Selena Barnes," I shook his hand "And no, sorry I've never heard a thing about you."

After a few hours of him talking, I learned exactly how rich he was, what clothes he always bought and the types of foods he ate. In all honesty, he was a snobby jackass and I wanted him to shut up and drink. I said little about myself and that's how I wanted it. Though he was gorgeous, I wasn't looking for a soul-mate, so his preferences meant nothing to me.

After his beautiful brown eyes took on a glassy appearance, out of nowhere, he'd said, "I abhor all things paranormal. Those cretins sicken me with their claims of being vampires, werewolves, witches and the like. Did you know that some of them even believe they are demon hunters? I think they're all just bottom feeders looking for attention."

This was highly amusing to Shawn and he slapped his silk-trousered leg as he laughed and laughed at people he knew nothing about. If he only knew he was currently in a town of 'cretins'! Inside, I cringed at his loathing for the people I'd known all my life, but I only needed him for a few hours of fun, so I sat in my seat and said none of the things that were itching to fly out of my mouth. Sure, I could've had sex with any available man in town, but I knew all of them and all of the single guys were looking for more than I was willing to give them. So, I kept reminding myself that I just needed a 'hot body' for a few hours of fun, that was all.

As the night wore on, Shawn became good and sloshed. I knew if we didn't leave soon, he'd be passed out at the table and I'd still be angry and horny.

"Wanna get outta here, Mr. Moneybags?"

"My place or yours?" he slurred.

"Yours, of course. I never take a guy to my home on the first date."

My parents would've flipped! Besides, I knew if things got out of hand with Shawn, I could hold my own. I always carried a knock-out potion in my purse. Regardless of a person's size, that concoction would bring a person to his or her knees. At the time, I was always protected and cautious.

He'd been so drunk that a bouncer had to help me get him to my car. A few moments after we pulled out of the parking lot, gone was the mouthy, self-righteous pig I had met only a few hours before. In his place was a man like any other man, snoring loud enough to raise the dead, fast asleep in the front seat of my car.

"Now, isn't this every woman's dream?" Luckily, I knew how to rouse him from slumber.

I drove him to his hotel and with the night janitor's help carried him into his room. Not ready to return home, and maybe because I was determined to get laid, I undressed and crawled into bed beside his still form, I conscientiously placed a condom package on the nightstand within reach.

I trailed kisses along the side of his neck as I pressed my full breasts against him. Shawn murmured his approval and I slid on top of him. His silk tie proved tricky to untie so I loosened it, and slipped it over his head. It took every ounce of patience I possessed to carefully unbutton each of the pearl buttons of the expensive but now wrinkled shirt he wore. Sure, he could obviously afford a new shirt if I ripped it open, but I wasn't a total bitch.

At the touch of my hands upon his chest, which was much more defined than I would have guessed from a business man stuck in an office all day, Shawn stirred and slowly opened his eyes. "What? *Mmm*…Selena? Where am I?"

"Yeah it's me." The last thing I wanted was for him to ruin the moment by talking. I silenced him with a kiss. I sensed a moment of reluctance from him before I sucked his bottom lip into my mouth, nibbling lightly while my hands roamed across his shoulders and arms.

To my elation, our kisses grew more passionate and the man showed he knew how to work his tongue. He slipped it into my mouth, teasing and searching. His hands gripped my ass and I rotated my hips against his Armani-clad erection. The sheer decadence of rubbing my swollen and slick folds across such fine clothing only heightened my arousal. I no longer cared about messing up his clothing.

Shawn rolled me over without breaking our kiss. He pushed off of me long enough to shed and toss his suit jacket and shirt. They landed across the room on top of an oak table and he collapsed on top of my eager body.

"*Mmm*, what are these awful things between us? You've got me at a disadvantage, lover." His upper body was amazing, smooth and hard but I needed more.

He stood to remove the offending trousers and I perched on my knees, licking, kissing, touching every inch of his available, exposed skin. The scent of his cologne mixed with his unique 'man' smell drove me wild. There was an undertone of freshness that reminded me of a day spent out on the ocean or walking the beach and it mingled with the scent of sexual desire. There was no other way to describe it, it belonged to him, and it was him.

I was surprised by the size of his manhood. Based on his hand size, I'd assumed I was in for a real treat. Sadly, that wasn't the case. But I was too far gone to stop.

"I need it now." I pulled him to the bed, pushed him onto his back and sheathed him with the latex barrier for our protection before I straddled his hips. Already primed, I guided his cock to my mound and slowly eased my hips down inch-by-inch until his shaft settled inside of me.

"Selena, you're so beautiful, so tight."

"Thank you, now please…fuck me. I can't do this alone."

On the edge of euphoria, I hoped he would remain coherent enough to follow through. To my surprise, Shawn arched his hips and met me thrust for thrust. I bounced up and down, smashing my clit against his pelvis as he held onto my breasts, squeezing and thumbing my rosy nipples. An almost painful heat shot to my core as my first orgasm ripped through me and I slowed the pace in order to milk the moment as my muscles squeezed and released his cock.

"Yes! Come baby, come," he shouted beneath me.

Not to be rude, but I found it distracting. I've never been into the whole 'screaming' and 'dirty-talk' thing. I lost all sense of rhythm and practically watched the remainder of my climax walk out the door. With reluctance, I continued the romp for Shawn's benefit. His touch suddenly seemed annoying and no matter what I tried, I couldn't enjoy myself. Shawn slammed into me over and over again and I made the appropriate noises when I could. How he couldn't tell my crotch was dry or how uninvolved I'd become, astounded me. Shawn mistook my whimpers for moans and continued to try to shove his flaccid dick into me as hard as he could. The alcohol he'd consumed was affecting all of his abilities. I rode it out so to speak and sent up a silent prayer for him to finish quickly so I could get out of there as soon as possible. After another agonizing twenty minutes, he finally got it up long enough and came. I swear the man squealed like a hog rooting in mud!

Exhausted, disgusted and raw down under, I climbed off him before his semi-hard dick pumped out all of his seed. He didn't seem to care. In fact Shawn appeared content with our encounter and smiled as I stood to dress.

"That was great. We should do it again after I shower."

"Yeah, sure." I wasn't interested.

Thankfully, he didn't see me roll my eyes. I didn't want to seem like a bitch, but I hadn't had sex in over eight months and felt I deserved an amazing night. Instead, I wound up feeling cheap, ripped off and unfulfilled. When Shawn padded into the bathroom to flush the used condom and wash up, I took the opportunity to grab my clothing and sneak out of his room. I took the stairs two-at-a-time and in case he tried to stop me, I ran down the back stairwell and around the long way to my car.

"Maybe he won't even notice. Seems kinda self-absorbed, anyways." I mumbled

The entire night had been one of the biggest mental and physical disappointments I'd ever had. I drove home while the entire evening replayed in my mind. After the twenty minute drive, I arrived at our cabin around five in the morning. I showered with the hope of removing any physical reminder of the tawdry encounter with Shawn and pulled on my most comfortable cotton pajamas.

Grateful my parents were asleep, I tiptoed into our cozy kitchen and made a cup of tea from my own secret blend of herbs. The heady concoction did its job and I collapsed into my own bed eager for sleep to claim me. Neither the sad excuse for sex, nor Shawn Richardson ever appeared in my dreams that morning and I slept until the late afternoon.

After our night together, Shawn showed up at my home the following evening.

"How did you figure out where I live?"

"I asked around. Everyone knows you, Selena."

"But why?" I couldn't believe this man had the gall to come looking for me. "Who do you think you are? Can't you take a hint?"

I stomped upstairs and watched out my window as he pulled out of the driveway.

"What a pompous jerk!"

He came to our house every day for two weeks straight. He'd even gotten our phone number. Sometimes he called in advance, other times he didn't. It didn't matter if I didn't answer the phone and my protests at his impromptu arrivals went seemingly unheard. We'd have the same argument over and over again.

"You're clearly a psycho. Look, I know you think you like me or something. But I don't like you. Get over yourself already."

"I'm determined to win you over, Selena, and will do so by any means necessary."

He tried buying me both expensive and inexpensive presents, sweet-talking me and goading me into front-yard confrontations.

"I just want to see you. That isn't so bad, is it? Isn't it obvious I'd do anything for you?"

Every moment together was passionate in one form or another and I'd never met a man as infuriating and complex as Shawn was. He could make me laugh at his antics and make me yell in frustration within minutes of the former, and sparks were always flying in one way or another between us. After a few weeks, my initial irritation with the man and his lack of sexual prowess didn't seem important anymore. He'd broken my resolve.

No one was perfect. True, he wasn't as well-endowed as I'd hoped, nor did he know how to use his equipment, but maybe those things didn't really matter. His personality started to grow on me and I figured the universe had sent him to me for a reason. Shawn proved to be nicer than any man I'd met in a long time. And I found myself falling, falling hard for this Casanova.

Yes, he had his faults but who was I to judge him based on physical inadequacy and hatred for things he didn't understand? In time, I hoped I could educate him in both areas. Besides, I had faults and weaknesses of my own and I still hadn't told him I was a witch, even though my parents didn't approve of him. I was scared I'd lose him, lose how he made me feel and I didn't listen to anyone except Shawn. I was in love and so very blinded by him.

He treated me like a princess and catered to my every whim. It became my goal to be the perfect girlfriend. I stopped being so sarcastic and I never told him he could or couldn't do something. When my parents were spell-casting or cooking up potions, I met Shawn in town. He seemed to accept my eagerness even when it was under the guise of being the 'good girlfriend and taking turns'. I was completely malleable in every way. If there was a chance for me to make him happy, I jumped at it. Shawn was an amazing, sexy, intelligent, caring man and I found I truly liked him. I feared any upset would send him into the arms of another woman just as easily as he'd fallen into mine. His carefree spirit and kindness won me over.

Living with my magically talented parents made it difficult to keep my secret, so I spent more time at Shawn's palatial estate. They disagreed with every decision I made concerning Shawn. To say my parents didn't approve of him was an understatement. They hated that I'd already neglected my heritage just to be with him twenty-four-seven. They believed him to be sneaky and sleazy. Mother said Shawn was only after sex. My father of course, would never approve of any man dating his precious little girl but he held back as often as he could.

On top of these issues they were even more upset with me the day I told them I'd thought about completely quitting the craft. I couldn't risk Shawn finding out.

"I just don't think I need it. Look, how long it's been since I last cast a spell or made a potion. I'm just fine. The paranormal world is just fine. I can help you occasionally. I just won't be here for rituals or spell-casting. I want a normal life."

My mother, who was always ready with a witty comment, was initially at a loss for words over my decision and her silence spoke volumes. She acted like I'd ripped out her heart and stomped on it.

"How can you even think about doing this? Where is your pride, your respect for our family?" She ran into the house and we didn't speak for over a month.

Until that day, my life had always been about making everyone else happy and making my parents proud. My mother could not fathom why I'd now insisted on choosing Shawn over them.

"I can tolerate just about anything, Selena. However, I cannot understand the fascination you have with this man who wants you to turn your back on your heritage, your birthright. You're like a butterfly, flitting to and from one man after another. I know you love the attention, but this is taking it a bit too far, don't you think?"

"He doesn't know of my 'birthright', Mother. I can't tell him."

"Then why are you with him? You must know he is not 'the one'. After all of the boys you've met, you have to know there are plenty of others out there. You need to embrace your gifts and see him for what he truly is."

No, I wasn't a slut and I didn't sleep with every man I met. In fact, I'd only slept with a handful of men in my entire twenty-one years. But I did love the attention I received from most of the men I dated, at least for a little while. Once I tired of their clingy or demanding ways, I was off to find another. If I found one to suit my current desires, fine. If not, I didn't cry over it. I had plenty of other things to do.

I enjoyed spending time with my mom. She'd done a bit of demon hunting on a few occasions and I'd always loved to watch her prepare and cast spells to find them. Often, a demon could be eviscerated before anyone in town had suspected there'd been one. Some days, we'd work up some potions or spells to help people in town or just hang out together watching old black-and-white movies. I even enjoyed being by myself once in a while. There wasn't a need for a man unless I wanted sex and even then, I could manage that by myself, too.

Until I met Shawn, I saw my parents on a daily basis. Nine times out of ten, I was home to help my mother with supper, Sunday through Thursday night. But suddenly, trips with Shawn to exotic destinations and spur-of-the-moment dinner reservations kept me busy and away from home, away from them. They couldn't understand the sudden changes in me. I'd become someone else, someone they felt was a stranger and our arguments occurred more often.

"You barely know this man, Selena. How can you give up everything you are for a man you just met?" My mother pleaded with me to think things through and take it slow with Shawn, but I refused to listen and instead became defiant whenever the subject of Shawn was mentioned.

"I love him! Why can't you understand? This behavior is ridiculous. I can't understand why you hate him!" The talks would end with me tearful and my mother silent as I slammed the door and left.

Time spent with my father was often spent in silence and very uncomfortable so I avoided him as much as possible. "You're breaking her heart. I hope this man is worth it."

I believed they were smothering me, not wanting me to grow up. Occasionally, I even thought they were jealous of the love Shawn and I shared. They even threatened to tell Shawn of my deception, claiming he needed to know the truth. I'd throw an enormous, immature fit and heated words would be exchanged. We stopped speaking to each other to avoid confrontation and never reconciled before the night they died.

To this day, my parents' absence tore at my heart. How could I have been so horrible to my parents? As time passed, I realized they'd only wanted what was best for me. If only they had been able to see how wonderful Shawn was to me, but they died before they could get to know him better. They died thinking I hated them and they were both so mad the last time we spoke. I only hoped Summerland has taken away the anger they felt for me before their deaths.

I often thought about, as well as relied upon; the whimsical but true stories of Summerland my mother told me when I was a little girl. Whenever someone in our town passed away, she would recite the ancient lore of our paranormal version of Heaven and those tales calmed my spirit and gave me hope. She said there were many realms and many possible outcomes, but those who die are happier there than they ever were on Earth.

After their deaths, I often dreamed they were looking down on me, watching over me from the after-life. I hoped they were proud and at peace. I knew one day I would find out for myself, but for the time being I could only imagine. Some days, it was harder to think about. The guilt I carried was almost as heavy as the weight of the many questions I found myself wishing I'd asked. I've learned that not knowing all of the answers is one of the most difficult things to accept in life.

The only thing that helped soothe my wounded spirit was the hefty inheritance my mother left for me. I've never been materialistic and money could never buy my happiness, but I needed it as an insurance policy. That money gave me financial security in the event I ever ended up single again so I tried to spend the bare minimum when I bought my necessities. I even learned how to clip and use coupons, which helped to further discipline my spending habits.

My first and single significant purchase to date was a new place to live in after my parents died. I bought a large parcel of wooded property and hired contractors to build a wonderful, hill-top cabin nestled on the far side of the mountain for Sterling and me. We were far enough out of town to have privacy but not too far away if we needed something from the grocer. The cabin became the one place I could always find complete solitude. Every day I woke up feeling refreshed and peaceful. It was the only place I could truly be myself.

Four months after Shawn and I began dating, my parents died when their house exploded. The Council of Elders declared it a "magical accident," a spell gone wrong. Considering how my parents and I had left things between us, I was beyond consolation. After that, I decided the universe was telling me I'd made the right choice by hiding my magic from Shawn. The fact that I hadn't been practicing my craft for months proved I had some inner voice that kept me from dying with my parents, but the guilt of not being with them sometimes tugged at my heart. So many times I foolishly thought I could have saved them. I convinced myself if I had been there, maybe they would still be alive. Shawn stayed right by my side, comforting me through my grief and the dark days that followed, doing his best to convince me how ridiculous I was for thinking such thoughts.

"See why I hate the paranormal and those who claim to be, cupcake? The investigators have told the newspapers your parents were performing magic. Of all things! Can you believe the authorities are falling for this craziness? Your selfish, unstable parents thought they could perform magic and look what happened? They showed complete disregard for anyone but themselves, especially not thinking about you. I would've lost my mind if you had died because of their carelessness."

I couldn't believe my ears! It took all I had to not show him some magic right then and there.

"Selfish? Unstable? Are you serious? My parents are dead, Shawn. How can you be so insensitive? You seem awfully unstable to me, right now! Who says things like that? You may think they didn't like you, but they were just scared of losing me, scared of me growing up and leaving them. And that doesn't give you the right to bash them or their beliefs when they aren't here to defend themselves." I stood there looking at the man who claimed to love me. He was a stranger. How could he be so thoughtless and cruel?

"Selena, I only meant..."

"I don't care what you meant." I shrugged away from his outstretched arms, avoiding his embrace as I wept and again wondered what the hell I ever saw in him.

He pleaded with his huge brown eyes and his broad shoulders fell in defeat. "I'm so sorry, Cupcake. You're right. I'm a jerk. I had no right to say those things. I understand you're under an incredible amount of stress and I had no intention of creating more for you. Please let me hold you and love away your sorrows? You mean everything to me and I cannot bear to see you angry. Trust me, I never meant to upset you like this. Please forgive me?"

Against my better judgment, I was sucked in by his sorrowful, brown eyes. I never could stay angry at him. As he worried his bottom lip, pleading for me to understand he had meant no harm, I inhaled his crisp clean scent and fell into his arms, crying again. I hated arguing with Shawn and I avoided causing any confrontation with him, folding under pressure more times than not. Shawn had many faults but who was I to judge? I already knew how he felt about magic and there I stood before him, a liar. Which was worse—an opinionated, ruthless man, or a liar? I had no idea. Was one more offensive than the other?

He scooped me up in his strong arms and carried me to his room, apologizing over and over for his crass behavior, showering my face and forehead with warm kisses. We spent the rest of the evening alternately making love and cuddling. Somehow, my anger and sadness had become an aphrodisiac for me, spurring my libido into sexual overdrive. I couldn't get enough of his touch, the way he tasted and how wonderful he fit inside me. As soon as I would look at him or run my fingers through his silky, dark brown hair, I became aroused all over again. Shawn whispered words of adoration and comfort all night long, promising he would never say those things again. Shortly before dawn, I ran out of tears and energy. I fell asleep on his broad, tanned chest as held me in his embrace.

When the weekly newspaper filled the front page with details of the horrible explosion and the state arson investigator's findings, Shawn went off on another rant. "This entire town lives in a fairy-tale. Half of them think they are paranormal and the other half acts as though it isn't happening right under their noses! I say they should get rid of the crazies, lock them up and the rest of us can live a normal life!" He'd spread his arms wide, shouting with such ferocity, he looked maniacal. His face was a mask of sheer hatred and not for the first time, either. I'd become used to these tantrums of his and they no longer fazed me as they did before. I just didn't care. I knew he'd forget all about it in a few minutes, so I busied myself with staring off into space and blocked him out of my mind.

He had no idea what it meant to be paranormal. It wasn't simply a choice but I allowed him to believe it was. I knew he was ignorant of our ways, but I couldn't hate him for it. He was all I had left in the entire world except for my familiar, Sterling. I was determined to hold onto both of them for dear life. At the time, I was too numb to be angry at the many things Shawn said and by the time I was over the majority of my grief, I decided he'd been right. He was acting out of concern and love for me, how could I hold that against him? If it weren't for Shawn, I would've been living in their house when it exploded. I'd be dead. I justified my lies by telling myself lying had saved my life. Ever since then, I have fought the urges and cravings to tinker with my magic, but I long since had lost any urge to fight or argue with Shawn. I'd had enough sadness and at the time, I couldn't bear the thought of losing him, too.

* * * *

This is what happened every time I came into town. I was bombarded with thoughts from the past. It seemed like my mind's way of dealing with unfriendly episodes was to remind me of my beginning with Shawn, confirming to me that I did indeed have someone who loved me. After all, he'd stuck by me through the most terrible thing that had ever happened to me. Isn't that what everyone wanted out of life? Someone who loved them and in turn who they also loved? To me, it was the only thing that mattered.

Chapter Three

Maybe it was my nerves after the run-in with Janice or another bout of those wonderful, pre-wedding jitters, but I really needed a drink. I'm sure my pressure cooker of a car also played some role in my desire to imbibe, and I may not have been thinking clearly. Perhaps, I simply yearned for the illusion of friendship? Even if I sat at a table alone, drinking in a room of complete strangers, at least it meant I'd had a drink with someone other than myself. I hadn't been inside Tooth & Nail in years and I hoped the customers would be kinder than most of the townspeople I was used to.

For over a century, Tooth & Nail has been our town bar. It has withstood the wrath of Mother Nature, time, the economy and magic. I'm not saying anyone would ever try to destroy the bar with magic, but there have been a few instances of drunken sorcery in the establishment's long history. Tooth & Nail has mustered through it all and has been a haven of sorts for all humans and paranormals. The bar is a reflection of the way the town and our community has fought tooth and nail to coexist peacefully. The owners have always adhered to a strict policy of "No fighting, biting or hexing." In fact, the walls were adorned with many signs announcing this zero-tolerance code of behavior. If anyone were ever to ignore these rules, they were barred for life. Zero-tolerance means just that and there are no exceptions.

I stepped out of my car and into the afternoon sun and enjoyed the slight breeze which carried the comforting scent of our town along the Ohio. Contrary to popular belief, the river didn't stink of dead fish. In fact it was quite the opposite, thanks to a group of earth-loving witches, our water always smelled clean and fresh like rain.

"Despite how most people feel about me, I truly love it here." I meant every word I said as I made my way across the parking lot.

I pushed open the warded, wooden door and entered the familiar haven I used to call my second home. "It hasn't changed a bit," I whispered to myself.

The neon signs were lit, the spotless tongue-and-groove floor and the handmade antique bar top gleamed like new. As I showed myself to a table, I was greeted by a few people saying 'hello' and 'good to see you'. I smiled back and spoke to each of them before sitting down in a leather-upholstered booth with a hard-grained wooden table-top.

Inside, I felt giddy. I practically bounced as I sat there. The people here were actually speaking to me. Speaking to me nicely! I smiled as I let out a deep sigh of relief. I knew there had to be a glimmer of hospitality left in our wonderful town and I'd found it! It felt like a weight had been lifted from my shoulders, at least for a little while. I prefer to call it the calm before the storm.

Kelly Jacobs warily approached my table without even a hint of a smile upon her face. She's one of the many people who turned their back on me over the years, and it was apparent her feelings about me hadn't changed. As she stood there glaring down at me with her pen poised to take my order, it amazed me that we'd ever been friends. She looked like a complete stranger. Gone was my partner-in-crime and class-skipping buddy. She had been replaced with this woman who had large green eyes filled with contempt.

"What'll it be?" she asked with indifference. Clearly, she was only asking because it was her job to do so.

"A bottle of Coors Light, please." I said quietly.

She turned on her heel and walked behind the bar to retrieve my beer, brought it to me in record time, set it on my table and walked away without another word.

"Okay, that went well," I raised the bottle to my lips and took a long swallow of the ice-cold, golden elixir.

Thinking back on how things used to be, I got caught up in the memories of wonderful times with my former best friend. Kelly and I shared many classes in high school. Though we weren't stellar scholars, we made it through. She and I were on the Salem Ridge Panthers cheerleading squad, which offered various opportunities for socializing and nine out of ten times, our social lives trumped any studying that might be necessary. Every adventure we had together was always well worth any trouble we got into.

So many nights we had snuck out to party at the county line where kissing boys was the main event. Other nights, we could be found practicing magic on the very property where I now lived. Kelly didn't have any powers, per se, but she was always right there.

"That's it. You've got it! When will you teach me, Selena?"

"Teach you what? A love spell?"

"Hell, I'd settle for a shampoo recipe. We both know I'm not great at anything other than running, but I bet I could handle a simple potion."

She was a quick learner and soon we were gathering our ingredients and preparing them as needed. Each of us always had a new, pure shampoo or soap to use.

The few 'trickster' potions that we created were my idea and they didn't always work. More times than not, my brilliant ideas got us into trouble with my mother.

"How many times have I told you that you cannot perform magic in front of others, Selena? What if someone had been hurt?" Mom would firmly admonish me in front of Kelly or whoever my target had been, but once we were behind closed doors, she would always teach me the proper way to create any potion I desired.

Sadly, Kelly outgrew her fascination with potions and I was left to doing that work on my own for the most part. However, she loved watching me work magic and just like any best friend, she was always willing and ready to accompany me whenever I set off for our secret spot in the woods.

"It's like watching a goddess," she'd say with a dreamy quality in her voice.

I would just laugh. She could be so very dramatic and I knew she was just trying to appeal to my ego, but that's what friends do.

Shortly before graduation, Kelly acquired the ability of stealth. She could sneak up on anyone, anytime, and it started to freak me out. I would be all alone in the woods and suddenly there she was, watching me. Kelly never said a word. She simply stared as if she was observing my soul, waiting for something to happen. Instead of walking with me through the woods, she went running and hiking by herself at all hours of the night. There were countless rumors that she had become involved with black magic and running with a *wild* crowd of kids. I knew Kelly would never be into black magic, her heart was too pure, but I couldn't make sense of anything she was doing. She wouldn't talk to me about what was going on in her life and before I could do anything to stop it, we drifted further apart.

I would call her house, but she wouldn't come to the phone. I'd stop by and every time, her dad said she was busy.

Mr. Jacobs wouldn't offer any explanation. "I prefer to stay out of it."

Her behavior became very weird and it finally started to scare me to the point that I'd try to avoid her. Sometimes, when I had no escape and would pass her in the hall at school or at the store, the look in her eyes was almost primal, full of hatred and something else I couldn't put my finger on. She obviously had some sort of an issue with me, but I had no idea why. After so many futile attempts at bridging our suddenly discordant relationship, I came to the conclusion she'd tell me when she was ready. I couldn't force her. Besides, all friends have disagreements once in a while, right? I only wished I knew what had caused ours.

The distance between us grew to mammoth proportions after her mom and two of her older brothers were killed in a hunting accident at their vacation cabin. I never heard the details, but I knew it was gruesome. Kelly's father sent his only living son, Keith, to work in Tennessee for some Wildlife Protection Program in The Great Smoky Mountains. Honestly, this didn't come as such a shock. I knew they had family spread across the country, but most of their relatives lived in Tennessee. Everyone knew the Jacobs were huge environmentalists and belonged to many groups, most of which sheltered injured and abandoned animals. So, sending Keith to the Smokies made perfect sense. After all, Kyle was suddenly a single father who was also grieving the loss of his wife and other children.

Kelly was kept under a very watchful eye by her father and he rarely let her out of his sight. This, in all actuality, wasn't much different from the way Kyle had treated her before their loved ones had died. But to me, it seemed as though the remaining Jacobs family members were hiding from the world. My insecure side thought maybe they were hiding from me? Of course, that wasn't a logical thought. But I missed all of them terribly. And I chided myself for even making any part of it about me.

I never understood why I was suddenly *persona non grata* and I got tired of asking. I didn't even hear from Kelly or her brother

Keith when *my* parents died. Part of me wanted to reach out to them, to anyone, but the other part of me said, *why bother?* They apparently wanted me to leave them alone and I wasn't going to beg anyone for friendship. I shouldn't have felt like I had to. The remainder of my so-called friends turned their backs on me with record-breaking speed as word of Shawn's and my engagement spread. Except for Shawn and my familiar, Sterling, I had been on my own the past four years.

Shaking my head, I realized I had been staring at Kelly while lost in thought and I noticed her watching me like a cat from across the bar. I sipped my beer and averted my gaze as I looked around at the few customers scattered throughout Tooth & Nail, sitting at the various tables and booths. There weren't many people and frankly, I was surprised. After a moment or two, I surmised that most of them were out and about with their families enjoying the warmer than usual weather. After the harsh winter we'd had, the heat was definitely a welcome change and everyone was ready to get over their cases of cabin fever.

Over the noise of the jukebox, I heard what sounded like an argument between one particular customer seated on a barstool and Kelly. I couldn't see who the man was, his back was to me. But every few seconds, Kelly would peek over the top of his head and then look back at him as she spoke in hushed tones. It didn't take a psychic to know the conversation was about me and obviously a serious one. Apparently, I couldn't even have a beer without making tongues wag. I might as well know what I was accused of having done now, so I slid out of my booth and walked to the front of the bar.

"It's none of your business, Kell," the man said, shaking his head from side to side before he took another drink of what looked like a soda.

As I approached them, I was already prepared to insert my two cents. The man, even from behind, felt familiar somehow and I felt the hairs stand up on the back of my neck. The air seemed charged with electricity, causing gooseflesh to crawl across my skin. I shook my head, warding off the chill that slid over me. I came to a stop directly behind the male customer, meeting Kelly's fiery gaze with one of my own.

"Of course it is. Have you lost your mind?" Kelly's auburn hair with silver tips bounced in the sunlight coming through the picture window as she shook her head at the man. "She is engaged to *Richardson!*"

"Rub it in, why don't ya? Does that mean I cannot even go say *hello?*"

"I am not going to argue with you. This isn't the time or place."

"For what?" I peeked over the man's broad shoulder and asked, "You're obviously talking about me, and shouldn't I be privy to this conversation?"

Kelly's face turned pink, she grabbed a bar towel and grumbled as she rushed to the other end of the bar, clearly not pleased. The man turned to me, smiling. Keith Jacobs stood and picked me up in a huge bear hug as he spun us both in a quick circle while my flip-flops dangled. I hadn't been hugged like that in forever! And Goddess, it stirred a longing deep within me that sent shock waves to my very core. No one had been this happy to see me in a very long time. Every firm inch of his body was pressed up against my own and it was heavenly. Keith smelled of the outdoors, like hard work and fresh air, manly. There was no hint of cologne that cost hundreds of dollars, only Keith, pure Keith! Why was I suddenly thinking like that? Surely two months without sex wasn't enough of a reason to have those thoughts. But in Keith's arms, I fit, really fit, and I felt ashamed for noticing it. I knew Shawn loved me, but as of late, I'd felt more like his buddy than his fiancée and that was taking its toll on my emotions. And I had missed Keith so much! It was nice to see one person hadn't changed.

"Selena, it's so great to see you, darlin'!"

"Keith! When did you get back to town?" And why hadn't he called me? *Stop.* I silently chided myself. I wanted to enjoy the moment but my broken-hearted, inner child threatened to rear her immature head.

"Last year," he said sheepishly as he set me back on my feet. My body was now warmed by his touch inside and out and it immediately felt cold and begged for him to hold me again.

"Last year? Why haven't I heard from you? No one even told me you were home." My voice raised an octave. Keith had always stirred strong emotions in me and years later, he still had the same effect.

"I suppose *not.* I hear you're engaged to Mr. Smooth Talker and I saw you coming out of Janice's shop with a dress bag. So I assume the rumor mill wasn't wrong this time? Besides, I'm sure he wouldn't want a dog like me sniffin' around his territory."

"You're far from a dog!" I placed my hands on my hips and I realized how very much I'd missed Keith *and* Kelly. "Yes, I am engaged," I bragged, showing him the ring and reminded my amped-up hormones at the same time. "The wedding is in two weeks. Please say you'll come?"

Abruptly, he returned to his seat at the bar. I stood there, silent and uncomfortable as I waited for the response I knew was coming. It was the same response I'd heard from everyone I invited.

"Sorry Selena. I've got a ton of work to do around here. Dad and Kell really need my help."

"Yeah, it's a really busy place. I can see you've really got your hands full. That's okay. I understand."

I tried to keep the disappointment and bitterness out of my voice as I tossed five bucks on the bar for my unfinished beer. Truth is I've never been a great bluffer. I was always more of a "wear your heart on your sleeve sort of girl" and today, I had reached the limit on the amount of bullshit I could tolerate. Why couldn't anyone treat me like they used to? Was it really that difficult to just come to my wedding and support me, to be happy for me?

"Selena, it *really* isn't because of you. I'm just busy. There's a ton of inventory that has to be finished in the next two weeks," he said as he looked everywhere but at me.

I knew better. Keith was just like the rest of the town of Shawn-haters. "It was good to see you, Keith. Take care." I kissed him on the cheek and walked out of the bar, fighting back tears of frustration and disappointment. Just as I reached out to open my car door, I heard him behind me.

"Selena, wait." It was more of a command than a request.

"Why, Keith?" With my back to him I said, "I understand. I really do. Please just go back inside. I've got things to do."

"More wedding plans, right?"

I detected another hint of sarcasm and spun around lightning-quick to face him. "What's *that* supposed to mean?"

Keith hung his head down abashedly and kicked a small, round rock with the toe of his boot, making his six-foot tall frame look as if he'd shrunk into himself. His demeanor took on an almost boy-like quality, when only a second ago he had been an adult full of piss and vinegar. Now Keith remained silent as if he needed a moment to gather his thoughts before he spoke. Lifting his head slightly at an angle and staring at me with brilliant blue eyes, Keith ran a hand through his shoulder-length hair. Identical to his sister's color and shade, the sun glinted off the silver-tipped strands as he dropped his shoulders in a sign of defeat. In that moment he was so handsome, so much like the young man I used to know that I wished our previous words hadn't been loaded with tiny jabs. I had an overwhelming urge to punch him or kiss him and I couldn't decide which I should do. There weren't words to describe what being close to this man did to me. I was a complete mess inside.

"Yeah, more wedding plans. I'm running out of time and I have no idea why I stopped by to have a beer. I should've known better. It was obviously another mistake."

"Oh, I bet." Suddenly Keith seemed riled up again. Gone was the nice guy. "Mr. Money Bags will have a fit when he hears you were here today."

"Again, what is that supposed to mean? What's with all of these snide comments? I'm a big girl, Keith, I can go where I choose. I had a beer, big deal. I'm sure he's had beer on his business trip."

"I'm sure he's had more than just beer," he mumbled and quickly recovered by asking, "Business trip? What kind of business trip?" His eyes took on a serious look and his brow was furrowed. It seemed as though he was keeping his hands in the pockets of his jeans to stop himself from grabbing me. What had gotten into this guy?

I chose to ignore his jab. "Um, yeah." I backed up and shrugged. "Didn't the town gossip-mill inform you? Shawn's in Germany on a business trip. He's been there for two and a half months." With my arms crossed over my middle, I prepared for a litany of accusations about Shawn's infidelities and escapades.

"No. Actually that little tidbit was conveniently omitted by everyone I've talked to. You're still going to marry him even though he took off halfway across the world and left you alone right before your wedding? Wow." Keith shook his head and chuckled. "You've really changed."

"Of course, I'm marrying him. He is over there for *work*. His main goal has been networking and rounding up investors for the factory expansion. Everything he has worked on for years, has been to better this community. And what do you mean I've 'changed'? I'm the same Selena you've always known. The same Selena you ignored and treated like crap after I confessed my feelings for you to your sister. The same Selena you neglected to tell you were leaving and the same one you forgot tell when you came home. I'm not the one who changed."

I stood there, staring back at him, my eyes daring him to deny what I'd said. We both knew I was right, but where did all of that emotion come from? What happened to me just wanting to talk to friends, to have a drink and enjoy being out in town?

"In this day and age of technology, he had to *fly* over to Germany to network?" I could see his flamboyant eye-roll and he looked as if he would laugh himself silly at any moment. What the hell was wrong with this guy?

"Keith, what are you getting at? Just spill it already! What? More rumors of him having an affair? Is he the anti-Christ? Every week it's something new. So, please entertain me with your newest version of whatever it is my fiancé has done now. You have my full attention!" I placed my hands behind my ears bending them forward. "See, all ears, Mr. Jacobs."

Yeah, I knew I was being immature, but I really didn't give a damn. The people walking by, with their arms full of recent purchases, stopped to witness my latest public temper tantrum and I didn't even acknowledge them. Let them watch. Let them see how much I truly didn't give a shit anymore. Maybe then they would leave Shawn and me alone.

"The entire town can't be wrong, Selena."

"Whatever you say, Keith." I took a deep breath and climbed into my car for the third time on that crazy day, eager to go home where I was safe from public scrutiny. "It was nice seeing you, but I've gotta go. Take care."

I looked in my rearview mirror after I drove off. There he stood in the parking lot with his hands on his hips, shaking his head and staring after me. Why did I get the feeling Keith had a lot more to say? How could Keith know more information about my fiancé than I did? Why hadn't I just stayed and asked him that myself? Why did I always run away from the truth? Ironically, I had no idea I would come face-to-face with it sooner than I ever imagined and that truth would shake me to my very core.

Chapter Four

As I drove home, my thoughts were stuck on Keith. "Even he has turned against me."

I found it ironic that I'd once believed we were meant to be together. Now, I chalked it up to a school-girl crush. It seemed like more of a childhood infatuation for my friend's brother, nothing more. How could I have ever liked a guy who was so jealous and spiteful?

"How could I think we were destined to marry? I really don't even know Keith or anyone else at all, anymore. I don't think I ever did." I shook my head as if to clear the intrusive thoughts, full of shame as if it was a sin to even remember my feelings for an old friend. I was nowhere close to being a saint, but I knew my mind should only be full of thoughts about Shawn and me. Still, I couldn't help but think Keith must be jealous, just like the rest of the townspeople.

I rambled to myself the whole way home. "Why can't anyone just be happy for me or be there for me?" I knew I was whining and I hated it. For the first time in a long time, I questioned who I'd become. I wondered if Keith were right? I wasn't prepared to answer those questions and instead decided I could always drown my sorrows in Moose Tracks ice cream once I arrived home.

As I unlocked the front door to my cozy cabin, my familiar, a silver-gray cat acknowledged my arrival with a yawn. "Nice to see you, too, Sterling."

"It's about time you showed up," he said and stretched as I took the offensive mauve garment bag off of my dress, wadded it up and threw it away. Once my gown, sans the gaudy, pink wrapper, was safely ensconced in the living room closet, I felt much better.

"Well, excuse me. I thought cats were supposed to be solitary, self-sufficient creatures. So, what's up?"

"Your phone and computer have been driving me nuts! Every few minutes a call or an e-mail is chiming. How's a cat supposed to sleep with the racket around here?" he huffed indignantly.

"Did you ever think of turning the volume down?"

"Ha-ha. No thumbs, witch."

Sterling was extremely serious, but I had to fight hard to suppress the giggle bubbling inside of me as he stood on his hind legs and raised his front paws. He must've woken up on the wrong side of his kitty condo. Or maybe he'd had too much catnip and had a kitty hangover. With Sterling, it could have been anything.

"You know I can hear your thoughts, right?" He flipped his tail and narrowed his eyes into slits.

I bowed to him, mockingly. "How could I ever forget, your Highness?"

He followed me to the kitchen where I grabbed my pint of Moose Tracks from the freezer and he watched as I ate the decadent treat right from the container with a spoon. I know, I know. Ladies do not eat from the container, but I was seriously miffed and who was going to stop me? At least I thought to use a spoon. Besides, I only had a few more weeks of solitary living before I'd move into Shawn's palatial and sterile, factory-made home. "We really should have discussed him moving in here instead." I mumbled around a mouthful of chocolate fudge.

"Where were you?" Sterling demanded.

"I picked up my dress and then I stopped by Tooth & Nail. Why?"

"What were *you* doing at *Tooth & Nail*?" He stared me down like an Inquisitor reporter.

"Not that it's any of *your* business, but I had a beer and I saw a few people who actually spoke to me. Why? Is it against the rules, Great Master?" I laughed and licked my spoon clean.

"No need to be snippy, Selena. I simply noticed a distinct scent on you. Did you stop at the animal shelter?"

Placing the ice cream back into the freezer, I said, "Sterling, I told you where I was. I went to Always the Bride and then stopped by Tooth & Nail. That's all. Do you think I was out looking for a nice, cuddly kitten to take your place?" I joked.

"You would never!" Again he flipped his tail maniacally. I truly had ruffled his fur. "I swear I smell dog on you. You *reek* of dog. I'll never understand why humans love those hideous, drooling beasts. Yuck!" He visibly shivered and rolled his eyes.

"No. I did not see, hear or pet any dogs. Maybe your senses are overactive today? Janice didn't even have that annoying pink poodle with her at the shop. Maybe that's what you smell? I accidentally plowed into her and knocked her on her big, ole, pink butt when I arrived at the shop." Though it wasn't fun landing on the woman, it was fun to watch her heave herself back up.

"*Accidentally?*" I swore he wore an evil grin. I could picture him rubbing his paws together like a furry Austin Powers.

"Of course it was an accident. I was late. Thank the Goddess I don't have to go back there. My dress fits great, by the way. I'm surprised Janice didn't sabotage it. That woman's attitude is hideous! If the government ever instituted a personality transplant law, I'd have that woman at the clinic so fast..."

"She's a snake. What do you expect? She probably ate that poodle." He snickered. "No big loss, you understand. But the woman is an upper-level shifting demon and she prefers small dogs as snacks, not companions. You did know that, right?"

I rolled my eyes. "Of course I knew that." No, I didn't. But I wouldn't admit it to Sterling. How could I not know Janice was a demon? What the hell was going on? My inner alarms, my sixth sense, whatever, should've been ringing my ears off! And I had been around her so many times.

"I can still hear your thoughts. Anyway, I assumed you knew and chose to ignore it like you ignore everything else that happens around you." He walked away, leaving me a not-so-attractive view of his un-neutered backside.

Laughing, I gathered peppers, onion and sausage from the fridge. I had a serious craving for *Dirty Rice* and set about chopping the veggies and browning the meat. Once that was well on its way, I prepared a bowl of fresh tuna for Sterling and carried it to *his* dining room.

His kitty condo was an exact replica of my house and took up an entire back bedroom. From floor to ceiling, the miniature cabin was one of my largest investments. When I hired a contractor to install all of my secret cubby-holes and a small, secured room in which to hide my craft items, I also paid him to build Sterling a suitable retreat. I figured Sterling should have a place to go when Shawn came over to visit and it curbed Shawn's allergic reaction to Sterling at the same time. Most of the time, Sterling spent his days in his home while I tended to my garden or walked in the woods that surrounded my property. He was happy, Shawn was happy and that made me happy.

As I sat his bowl of tuna in his house, Sterling climbed his front steps and pushed open a tiny, wooden door. He climbed a carpeted stairway to his upper loft and then crossed over a cat-size deck overlooking a small fountain complete with a few Koi. Spoiled? Party of one? You bet! When it came to Sterling and his home, I often paid more attention to his needs than my own. But that's what pet owners do, right?

"*Bon appetit!*" I trilled in my poor French accent and bowed as I sat his plate of food on his deck. Sterling loved to eat beside his pond as he watched the fish swim by. If you asked me, I'd say he was being sadistic, letting them know they could be his next meal if he chose. He swore having the pond kept his inner spirit calm. *What-ev-er.*

Returning to my kitchen, I added the rice to my mixture of meat and veggies. I'd been making this newest addiction of mine once a week for the past six weeks. I blamed it on Mardi-Gras. "At least it contains most of the major food groups," I said to myself. "Wait. Are there even *food groups* anymore?"

"What's the deal? You've been eating healthy for weeks. If you ask me, it's making you edgy."

Startled by Sterling's stealthy behavior, I dropped the glass lid of the electric skillet onto the counter. "Boy, you're sneaky today!"

"See? You're edgy and jumpy. Maybe this wedding is getting to you? You can always call it off," he said as he washed his paws. "No one would blame you." His little pink tongue darted out of his mouth wetting each individual claw, ensuring every tasty drop of tuna juice would be history within seconds.

"Seriously?" I was at my limit and slammed the wooden spoon I'd been using on the counter. Of course, it broke in two. "Damn it."

"Mistress, everyone knows he's a fink! All day, every day, I hear the chatter. No one likes him except you." He switched to cleaning his tail as my temper flared.

"Why? They used to love Shawn. At least until we started dating. And what do you mean, you *hear* the chatter? You sit here twenty-four/seven holding the couch down." Okay, maybe I'd been a bit harsh, but I couldn't take any more Shawn bashing, not even from my best pal.

"Um, ouch. That was a bit rude. You know I need my beauty sleep and besides, you're mistaken. No one has ever liked him. They're all afraid of him. He controls the economy of this town, he controls everything and you've been too blind to see it. In the beginning, they pretended to like him because of *you* and for *your* benefit. I guess they thought you could change him. But once you gave up your powers, all hope was lost. Everything changed. *You* changed. Now, they think of you as an ally for his horrible plans."

"They're just a bunch of old busy-bodies who make things up because they are bored! He'd never hurt anyone and he isn't the raging sex lunatic they paint him to be. He saved this town from economic downfall many times and they repay him with spiteful viciousness! They're wrong."

"That's not what I hear from my associates." He hopped up on the counter, blinking at me innocent as could be, and straightened his spine.

"Associates? What associates? Are your catnip mice talking to you now? You sit here all day grooming and napping. How could you have associates?" I laughed at his superior demeanor.

"I'm not at liberty to divulge my sources or how I came to possess such information. Your fiancé is *no good.* That's all you need to know. And the sooner you see the truth, the better off all of us will be." With a huff, he jumped down from the counter and sauntered to his condo.

I had been dismissed by a sarcastic, mouthy cat who believes he is the know-it-all of the paranormal world. Being given the silent treatment by my last friend on the planet wasn't what I needed. Life was great.

* * * *

After dinner, I sat at my desk sifting through e-mails. Many were spam, offering life-changing results and a better life. Given the erectile dysfunction medication, burial insurance, Lasik eye surgery and *Shazam!* bra ads I received by the boatload every day, one would think I was a big, hot mess.

"If I was to die a suspicious death and the cops were to investigate my e-mails for clues, they would think I was a complete wreck and killed myself. A woman with saggy boobs, penis problems, researching sex changes, blind, single, depressed and in need of burial insurance with the perfect timeshare property! I'm a scientific miracle!" I laughed as I imagined our county detective's face as he scrolled through the various spam files looking for clues.

"You won't die anytime soon and you can't kill yourself. It isn't possible for a witch to commit suicide, you know that."

"Jeez, Sterling, again with the sneaking?" He sat at my feet again bathing himself. "Another bath? How could you have possibly gotten dirty?"

"Who's sneaking? I didn't know I needed to announce my arrival in my own home. Is that a new rule for everyone or am I the only one you require notice from?"

"Very funny. Exaggerate much? I know I can't commit suicide, that's not what I was saying. Besides, I'll be married soon, why would I off myself now? I said the police would *think* I did. These spammers are ridiculous. One says, *Anti-Depressants! Half-off!* And another says, *Single? Alone? Desperate? Open this email immediately!* Does anyone even buy any of this load of crap?"

"Probably. Was all of that, *you've got mail* business just a bunch of spam today? All of those bings and beeps gave me a migraine." Sterling still seemed a bit miffed, but at least we were on speaking terms again.

I snickered. Everything was always about Sterling and I loved his selfish side just as much as I loved his sweet side. "No. There are a few other normal e-mails, probably wedding related. They can wait. I'll get to those later."

He hopped up onto the desk, hovering beside me, nosey as could be. "That one says, *Urgent!* How do you know it's spam? I think you should open it."

"There isn't a sender's name on it. I'm not opening it. Besides, a lot of spammers use the term '*Urgent!*' It's a trick. My luck, I'll open it and end up with some type of computer virtual STD. I bet my e-mail will develop a life of its own and spam every contact I have. Hackers will do anything to get into computers." I could feel my heart race as I imagined the consequences of opening a shady

e-mail. They'd break down my door and haul me off to some
federal prison, never to be seen or heard from again! I'd end up in
some cell with a crazy lady who'd make me her pet. Oh hell, no!
The thoughts of those goddess-awful outfits, not to mention the
shoes. I thought I'd barf all over my desk, my palms were sweaty
and I couldn't breathe.

Rolling his emerald eyes, Sterling said, "Drama queen, party
of one? As if *you* are *that* important." He flopped onto his side
laughing. "Yeah, some weirdos are gonna funnel top-secret
information through *your* computer, setting you up to take the
heat! Are you serious? Ha-ha-ha-ha-ack!"

"Karmic hairball, Mr. McFuzzy Nuts? Who's laughing now?"
I walked to the kitchen, eager to be away from his teasing. I filled a
bowl of water for him after I poured myself a glass of wine,
thinking how foolish I'd been. I knew I'd over-reacted and knew I
should know better than to spaz about such trivial things.

To my surprise, when I returned I discovered that Sterling had
turned his nose up at my offer of a drink and remained at the desk.
I took a big gulp of merlot and consequently blew it everywhere
when I reached my comfy office and saw that Sterling had opened
the top-secret message! Thank the Goddess, the sticky alcohol had
only landed on the desk, but there, wide open, was that suspicious
e-mail.

"Oh great! If this computer blows up, you're buying me a new
one! What if the feds show up here thinking I'm the spamming
hijacker? Did you ever think about that?"

"Breathe, Selena. It's just an e-mail. It seems pretty important
and I really think you should read it." Sterling's voice had taken on
a much more serious tone than I'd ever remembered hearing out of
him before.

Okay, I admit I can be a bit of a drama queen. But in my
defense, I spend my days talking to a royal pain-in-the-ass and I
am a bit stressed with the wedding and all. Who wouldn't be
dramatic?

"I knew it! See, Mistress! Here's your proof." He scampered
back and forth across my desk as if he'd just found a *real* mouse
made of catnip.

"Proof of what? Move over fuzzy-butt, so I can see." And boy,
did I ever. On my screen was an anonymous letter—

Dear Selena,

You don't know me, but I've been assigned to watch over you. I have been in the shadows ever since your parents' unfortunate deaths. Though I'm sure you will have many questions, I cannot answer them at this time. You need only know this, your fiancé is cheating on you, again. There are many things about him you need to know. The danger you are in increases by the hour. I have attached proof because I know you will not believe me without it. Do what you will with this information, but understand you need to think clearly and realize how very serious this matter is. Your actions will be carefully monitored. I will be in touch.

"What. The. Hell?" I couldn't believe my eyes! Now people were claiming to be guardians of some sort and sending me emails full of lies? When would it stop? "I've had enough of this garbage for one day! Sterling, go to your condo, now! I don't want to hear a peep out of you."

Strangely, yelling at my familiar didn't make me feel any better. In fact, I felt like shit. I knew he had issues with Shawn, hell, everyone had issues with Shawn. But damn! How much more was I supposed to tolerate?

"We'll just move. That's it. If we leave town, they will have to leave us alone. We'll get married someplace else. Somewhere that isn't full of back-biting, conniving jerks! First, I'll call Shawn. I know he'll agree. I'll pack everything up and find us a suitable home. Well, find us a home and *then* pack. Whatever. As long as I can get away from here, everything will be fine. I just have to remain calm."

I knew I had to leave Salem Ridge *before* I used my magic. I'd had all I could take.

"Goddess, help us," Sterling muttered before scampering off to his room.

Sterling hid in his house, steering clear of me as I blew through the house on a cleaning spree. He knew I teetered on a very thin line and staying out of sight was probably the smartest decision he'd made all day. As I've mentioned, not using my powers for years was a very bad thing.

As I worked my way down the hallway with a mop, I heard Sterling say, "Lovely. Here we go." He hated the smell of my homemade cleaner and his disapproval was nothing new, nor did I care what he wanted at that point.

I only cleaned like a madwoman when I was angry, very angry. Most of the time, the house was spotless, so there was no need for heavy-duty housework. But I had to do something to expel the incredible energy that threatened to explode from my body.

After scrubbing my hallway, kitchen and living room from top to bottom, I sat down on my sofa hoping the wave of anger had truly receded. I'd become overheated and my temples were throbbing.

"It will be okay. No magic. No magic." I willed myself to calm down, taking deep, calming breaths. "In with the good, out with the bad." I knew if I opened the door to my powers it would be so very hard to close. There would be no going back.

Picking up my cordless phone, I dialed the international number for Shawn's hotel. I was one of the few people in the world without a cell phone. I didn't want or need one and I liked the feel of a real phone instead of some tiny, weak piece of plastic that I could easily break or lose. Shawn of course, had a cell but when I asked him why he hadn't answered my calls, he told me that his had crappy reception over there. Considering the time difference, I hoped he'd still be in his room at the early hour, maybe having his morning meal.

It took forever to be connected and it took all I had to suppress my irritation when the desk clerk answered and I requested to be connected to Shawn's room.

"Room 211, Shawn Richardson, please."

"Mr. Shawn is in a different room now. Hold, please." The nasally voice across the seas replied.

"He must've finally requested a larger room." I knew he'd been disappointed with the smaller room and he felt claustrophobic. Every time we spoke on the phone, he reiterated the same complaints to me. I'd mentioned switching rooms countless times, but he'd claimed to forget, got too busy or used whatever reason he could come up with. Sometimes, I swore he was one of those people who wasn't happy if not complaining about something. Strange that he'd waited until he only had two weeks left in Germany to change rooms, but oh well.

I again waited for what felt like an eternity to be connected. I needed to hear his voice. I had calmed down quite a bit and hopefully talking to him would help. At the moment, I was still undecided whether to mention the ridiculous e-mail or not. Part of me wanted to cry and share this latest attempt at destroying my dwindling comfort with him and the other part of me just wanted to forget it had happened. The only thing I knew for sure was that I couldn't take much more. In my own land of naivety, I had no idea how drastically my life was about to change. The e-mail was just the beginning.

Chapter Five

"Hello?" A woman purred. "Roberta and Shawn's Passion Palace, how may we help you?"

"Roberta? Roberta who? What..." Who the hell was answering my fiancé's phone?

"Get back in this bed, you little Irish wench!" Shawn giggled, yes, I heard *my* fiancé *giggle* in the background!

"Roberta, I don't know who you are but I'd like you to put Shawn..."

The phone disconnected. "The bitch hung up on me!"

I called back and the line was busy. "You've got to be fucking kidding me!" How the hell was I supposed to bitch and get to the bottom of this if they didn't answer the phone? Why there was some woman named Roberta in my future husband's room, I had no idea.

Maybe I'd misunderstood. Could I have heard the woman say Ron, John or something and only thought I'd heard her say Shawn? After all, I did have Shawn on the brain, so maybe it was all a huge misunderstanding?

I knew better. I'd heard it with my own ears. The woman answered the phone in Shawn's room, confirming years of rumors, truths and my worst fears.

"Roberta who? And who freaking says, 'so and so's Passion Palace' when they answer a phone? Who says *that*?"

I knew it wasn't some kind of sick, twisted joke. There was no way around it. When I heard Shawn tell Roberta to get back in his bed, I could've thrown up. For them to leave the phone off the hook was rubbing salt in a huge, gaping wound. They knew I'd call back. They knew I'd be pissed. I was officially a woman scorned and I had every right to cuss them out. How dare they take that privilege away from me!

For years and years I'd dismissed rumors about Shawn and it'd finally taken its toll. In the attempt to alleviate my own guilt over my own lies, I'd ignored every single truth they'd said about Shawn. And the worst part, I knew the entire town was right. I was a fool. The room spun and every story I had ever heard came crashing through my mind with the speed of a freight train. And just like that, I knew who the mysterious Roberta was. Roberta McManus, that dirty, nasty whore!

I felt anger for the first time in my life. True, homicidal anger. How could he do that to me? What had I done to deserve what he'd done? Who the fuck did he think he was?

"Screwing that old biddy of a woman! He could've at least picked someone half-way attractive!"

There was a buzzing in my ears. It felt like a warm whisper singing a lullaby and I found comfort in the madness I felt. It comforted me and I had no idea why, but I needed more.

"Selena, you need to calm down." Sterling was right behind me.

"Fuck calming down! Don't tell *me* to calm down! He's over there screwing *Roberta McManus!* Remember her? She's that ugly, old, frumpy bitch-of-a-woman who works with Shawn at the factory.*"

I really thought I had to be going crazy. Never in a million years would I imagine Shawn and Roberta sleeping together! *My* fiancé really was cheating on me! What made it worse was, with a woman who was disgusting and vile. Though I had only met her once, that one time was enough.

Last year, I'd met the home-wrecking whore. When we shook hands at a factory dinner party, I instantly disliked the woman and it took all I had to refrain from wiping her nasty hand sweat off on my skirt! She was so repulsive and acted like she was better than I was, with her snide, condescending manner. Every word she said was loaded with a blatant tone of bitchiness. It was one of the worst factory get-togethers ever and I couldn't wait to leave that night just to get away from her. A short three-hundred and sixty-five days later, I stood there deciding how to kill the slut.

So many thoughts raced through my mind as I tried to decide what to do, causing my head to pound like an Aborigine drum. I wasn't even crying. Over the past four years, I had spent so many nights crying over the rumors that ran rampant around town that now I was all out of tears. Shouldn't I have been a snot-covered, blubbering mess? Instead, I was pissed off! Did this prove I didn't really love Shawn as much as I thought I had? My feelings leaned more towards betrayal and embarrassment than those of a jilted love-sick bride-to-be. I swore at any given moment my forehead would explode and mental diarrhea would gush out everywhere, ruining my beloved hardwood floor.

"What the fuck? What the fuck? Sterling, what the hell just happened?"

"You know what happened. Selena, you finally faced the truth. The truth everyone has been trying to get you to see for four years. Now, please try to calm your thoughts. They're racing again and I can't handle all of it at once."

I stood there with my mouth hanging open, truly flabbergasted! *My* world just went to shit and *Sterling* had the nerve to complain about his discomfort? Seriously?

"By the gods Sterling, *please don't say another word.*" When I looked at him, he actually seemed frightened. Frightened of *me.*

"Now Selena, I meant no harm, but…"

"But nothing!" I roared and he ran from the room.

I walked over to my desk and clicked on the anonymous e-mail and read it again. When I double clicked the attachment, thirty pictures starring my very naked fiancé and his very naked whore-bag popped up on the screen. There was my fiancé screwing Roberta McManus!

"I'll kill him."

As I scrolled through the pictures, one in particular caught my eye. Roberta was grinning like Lucifer's bitch and taking it from behind while my fiancé plowed into her. Upon further examination, I realized something even more infuriating. Roberta wasn't simply a home-wrecking whore; she was also a demon. Her glowing eyes and sharp teeth were quite visible.

"Roberta is a troll? Sterling! Out here now!"

He scurried out of his room and onto my desk. As he looked at the photos with me, he couldn't hide his surprise. "Holy balls, Selena!"

"Nice choice of words."

"Sorry. Wow! It's about time. How did you miss this? I mean, we, how did we miss this?"

"*We* missed this because *I* haven't been using my powers. Hell, for all of these years I haven't even been wearing my crystal! How could I have been so stupid?"

"You wouldn't listen. Just calm…"

"Don't you dare say it!"

"Okay. Let's think." Sterling pleaded.

"Screw thinking! I'm burning his shit, all of it!"

"Now Selena, please wait. You can't…"

"Oh, yes I can."

My powers streamed through me, filling me with wicked desires. I wanted Shawn to pay and to pay dearly! After everything I had foolishly given up for him and the way the town had completely abandoned me, a simple amicable break-up was not going to satisfy me. I closed my eyes, inviting the magic to flow through me.

When I opened my eyes, the sight before me could have knocked me to the floor. "I'll be damned Sterling, look at this!"

In one particular photo, the photographer had captured another shot of Shawn's condescending smile that brought no light to his eyes as he pounded into Roberta once more. Hell, Shawn didn't even have pupils!

"Oh shit, Selena. This is bad, really bad."

"Yep. I've been sleeping with a demon, too. He knew all along I'm a witch! He allowed me to lie and carry on as if everything was normal. What a lying, fucking hypocrite! Acting as if he believed, cared for and loved me all this time! Why would he do that? Why did he want me powerless, without my family and alone? What could he possibly gain? He had to be after something, but what?"

I paced the floor while murderous thoughts battled with the miniscule bits of sanity left in my frazzled brain. Did it really matter what Shawn wanted? I would never help a demon! But I had. I had been bamboozled into being a part of every rotten thing he had done to the people in my town. Clearly, keeping me powerless was his way of controlling me. How long had he and Roberta been commiserating? So many questions about the last four years popped into my mind, but there was only one answer. I knew there was only one way to stop him.

"What are we going to do?" Sterling was pacing now, his normally sleek, gray fur now standing on end showing he was clearly agitated. His tail, now the size of a raccoon's, twitched furiously back and forth, side-to-side. I could see anger in his furry little brow and fear in his eyes. My familiar was a conundrum of emotion.

"The only thing we can do. We're going to send them both back to Hell."

"But Selena, if you use your powers in anger and for personal gain, the Council *will* come for you!" His green eyes bulged with alarm.

I knew Sterling was right. When they came for me, I'd be bound and powerless. They would make me stand before a jury of my peers and I'd be found guilty of misusing my magic. The Elders would call a mystic who could bind my powers, sealing them inside my crystal pendulum. I'd be forced to wear the glowing, blue orb around my neck, showing the paranormal world I was convicted of crimes against them. Everyone would know what I had done.

There was only way for a witch to regain her powers. Mercy of the Elders would unlock the spell that bound a witch. If she tried to access her powers before the sentence was up, the witch would be thrown into a dungeon, deep below the earth. She would spend the rest of her living days, alone, and because witches live a lot longer than humans, that could be a very long time.

"It's too late. I've allowed the magic in. But maybe they will listen to reason after they've taken me into custody." I'd already accepted the inevitable. All I could do now was to finish what I started.

"We will think of something, Mistress." He rubbed against my ankles, trying to comfort me. "I won't let anything happen to you. But please don't do this."

"I can't believe I never saw the truth. Everybody tried to tell me. I wonder how many people knew he was a demon? "

"I have no idea. Honestly, you wouldn't listen. They tried to get you to leave him many times and it didn't work. It doesn't matter how many knew. The important thing is you know *now*."

"I still need to get rid of his things. I don't want him to have any reason to come back here, ever."

"No magic."

"Does it really matter at this point? I've already alerted them by bringing the magic back to life inside of me. There's no going back."

As the first wave of power raced through my body, I felt nothing except pure desire for more. More heat, more pressure, more everything. Every movement seemed to intensify my senses. Each sensation crashed over me in enormous waves of ecstasy, I had never felt such intense pleasure. I found myself wishing I had embraced it sooner.

I walked through my home scorching every photograph of Shawn and me that was still hanging. The simple act of imagining him burning quickly set the pictures aflame and melted his fake, sorry-assed smile out of existence. With a flick of my wrist the remaining photos flew off the walls, they were swirling around me as I made my way to the bedroom. They hovered, as if on invisible threads, dancing, and I watched them with a detached sort of pleasure.

My mother had told me secrets and spells for everyday living, and right then, more than ever, I was glad I could still hear her voice in my mind. *In order to break an emotional or spiritual bond with someone, you need to burn their personal belongings and anything you may have shared. Everything belonging to them must be returned to the ashes from which it came.*

At the time, it seemed like another lesson meant to drive me nuts with boredom. But I *had* listened, storing it away in the recesses of my mind along with the many other tidbits of knowledge she gave me. Now I understood what my mother had said. Somehow she knew I would need lessons like this one later in life. "I should have listened to her about Shawn. She saw right through him."

I snatched Shawn's clothing off of hangers and out of drawers, every last bit of it as well as the floating photos. Gathering the items in my arms, I carried the loads into the bathroom. Dropping everything into my oversized, pure copper bathtub, I snapped my fingers and mentally willed the items to burst into flames. "*So it is, so shall it be.*" In mere seconds the entire pile was nothing more than ashes.

I heard thunder rumble in the distance and for a fleeting moment, I thought it was strange. No severe weather had been predicted, so I continued about my business. Again, the storm outside announced its approach. Though my element is air, I was too distracted to connect any of the elemental dots.

"Selena, you're creating a storm. You need to stop before it's too late." Sterling was clearly concerned for my well-being, but I didn't care. I wanted power, more and more power.

"No, Sterling. Stopping is what I never should have done in the first place." My voice no longer sounded like my own. Somewhere deep inside, this should have struck me as odd, but instead I dismissed it. I went to the kitchen and gathered a dustpan and a trash bag.

Returning to the bathroom, I scooped all of the ashes into the bag. A quick look in the bathroom mirror showed the only physical change I harbored was in my eyes. Whereas before they had been brown, now electric blue orbs glared back at me. It barely registered in my mind before I raged on. Walking back through the kitchen, I opened the back door from ten feet away with a flick of my wrist and journeyed out into the woods surrounding my cabin. There were ten acres of primitive forest, so I had to walk quite a distance to find the perfect spot.

Lightning crashed and thunder echoed across the hill where my home stood, reminding me of the Civil War battles from over a century ago. I felt the fear, sickness and death of soldiers from centuries past surround me as I walked farther into the woods. A momentary flicker of fear passed through me as disembodied spirits flew through my body. The emotion was gone within seconds and it was replaced with orgasmic bliss as another wave of magic filtered through my veins, casting any remaining fear aside.

The power vibrated through my body, bringing a release that was one hundred times more satisfying than any sexual encounter I had ever had! My legs shook, almost buckling at the knees and still I craved more, needed more. Though it was dusk, I could see the gray and white clouds swirling above me as I walked barefoot over the land. Soft, rumbling thunder followed my every step as more magic built inside me. Arriving at a partially cleared area of the forest, I opened the bag of ashes. My mouth formed a small 'o' as I blew them into the wind I had created.

"Be gone from sight,
Be gone from sound,
Return to your place,
Beneath the ground.

So it is,
So shall it be."

Once the ashes disintegrated, I raised my hands to the sky, calling the wind to do my bidding.

Erase the scent,
Erase the mark,
Erase the hold
Upon my heart.
So it is,
So shall it be.

Thunder pounded and lightning crashed around me as an ice cold breeze blew through my bones. It painfully tore away any remaining claim Shawn ever had on me and I watched as green wisps of green, smoky haze lifted out of me, dispersing into the night sky. Light beams in various shades of black, red, and brown shot into me with the force of an EF3 tornado. I could feel myself being repeatedly lifted and set back down in place as each burst rocked through me, through my soul. I gave no thought to anyone or anything else. Each burst of power consumed my entire body, mind and spirit.

"Oh my Goddess!" My voice was raspy, barely more than a whisper and yet another thing about myself I no longer recognized. In the chaos that swirled around me and in me, I lost track of time and place. Hovering between the worlds of the living and the dead, I teetered on the brink of consciousness, surrendering to the unknown.

Beyond reprieve, I dropped to my knees as the last psychic parasite was torn from my body and replaced with something more. What that something was, I did not know. But it felt amazing.

"Take it all! I beg you! Fill me with whatever you choose, Goddess!" I shouted, using every last ounce of energy I possessed and collapsed face-down on a bed of leaves and dirt as the remainders of my echoing plea was smothered by the burning forest.

I'm so screwed, was my last conscious thought before the darkness claimed me.

Chapter Six

I slept for a short time and when I awoke in the pre-dawn hours, there were drops of rain pounding down upon my back. I was soaked and chilled to the bone. Spitting out leaves and dirt, I painfully rolled over, barely able to sit up. My head was throbbing with a force to rival any death-metal band. Every breath I took sent pain radiating through my entire body.

I looked around the vast clearing where once a beautiful forest of various trees had stood tall and proud. The rain continued to pour as if the stars themselves were weeping, clearly devastated by my actions. There was something wrong. I should never have been able to cause this much destruction. I'm a witch, but a good one. Where did the power I had used come from? Surely, there must be an explanation. Maybe I was still asleep?

I pinched myself as hard as I could. I gasped, inhaling quickly from the pain. The scent of death overwhelmed my senses. Smoldering embers were all that remained of my ten acre property. I had decimated everything.

"Sterling! Sterling!" I scrambled to my feet, fighting the urge to vomit as panic rolled through me at the same time. I ran through the woods, coming upon the rubble that only hours ago had been my home. It was flattened and charred. Little wisps of gray smoke plumed into the acrid air.

"Oh my Goddess! What have I done? Sterling!" I wailed into the silence.

Turning in circles, I saw only destruction around me. Falling to my knees again, I cried and cried as soul-wrenching sobs tore through my body. I rocked back and forth, holding my insides together for I was sure they were being ripped out with grief. "What am I going to do?"

"For one, you're going to stop that pitiful crying and get up!"

"You're right. I am pitiful, I should've listened to you and now I've killed you" I wailed again.

"Yes. You *should* have listened. Now, just look at the mess you've made. Lucky for you, I have eight more lives but that doesn't fix it. Do you have any idea how much it hurts to die and not to mention, the agony of coming back to life. Oh, and don't forget how horribly awful my fur looks! I look like death warmed over! It will take weeks before I feel or look like my old self again. Now, stop that god-awful sniveling and get up. We need to leave here as soon as possible. Bad things are coming for us. Very bad, Selena."

I looked up to find the most beautiful pair of green eyes glaring at me. "Sterling!" I scooped him up, holding his soaking wet body tight to my chest, I whined, "I'm so sorry," over and over again as I wept tears of joy. His protests were muffled as I continued to hug and kiss his charred little head. "It will grow back. I promise. You'll be handsome and good as new in no time! I'm so glad you're alive! Please forgive me?"

"Let go of me! I can't breathe, you blubbering ninny! Are you *trying* to kill me again?" He tapped my face with his furry, gray paw with the force of a slap and I dropped him immediately. "Now get it together, Toots! Didn't you hear a word I said? We have to get outta here and I do mean now!"

Sterling was right, but how were we going to go anywhere? I really wasn't capable of functioning yet. There were so many things I needed to process and I had no idea where to begin. I needed coffee to clear my foggy brain and unfortunately my coffee beans, grinder and brewer were all roasted beyond recognition. I sat in the debris and rubbed my pounding temples.

"Sterling, do you know where my crystal is?"

"Yes. When you went all apocalyptic, I snuck into the house and grabbed it. I hid it down by the creek in that huge tree those pesky squirrels love so much. There was a hole in the trunk, so I hid it in there. I tried to go back into the house to get your wallet, but that's when the house exploded and I don't remember anything after that."

"Will you please go get our pendulum? Maybe the crystal will help me gather my thoughts."

"Sure. As always, I'm here to serve *you*. Even though I only recently came back from the dead, I will just…"

"Sterling, not now." I watched as he scampered off into what remained of the woods, his tail pointing straight up in the air. "I will be kissing his ass for years after this." I shook my head, causing more intense streaks of pain to blow through my forehead.

As I sat there trying to come up with a plan to save our asses, I tugged on my ring. "My ring! Holy crap, I forgot to destroy the ring!" I pulled and pulled but the ring wouldn't come off! I slobbered like an idiot all over my finger and still it would not budge. This was bad. On a scale of one to ten, it registered at least an eleven. In my fury-driven frenzy I had forgotten to get rid of the one item Shawn and his troll would be able to track me with. The damn diamond. "Lovely."

"Here. You know you really should've gotten rid of that ring? He can track you through that and we will never be safe."

I caught the crystal and rolled my eyes at my ever helpful familiar. "Thanks so much Sterling. I hadn't thought of that!"

With dread and defeat, I looked down at my hand. The gold band had melded through my skin and into the bone of my ring finger! There was no chance I was getting it off anytime soon. Hell, before now I had never even attempted to take it off. For all I knew, it could've been unmovable for quite a while. "We are so screwed. The Council and demon-boy are going to have to fight each other to see who gets the privilege of ripping us apart."

I slipped the crystal pendulum over my head and the weight of it felt more solid than anything had in years. I could feel and see its calming properties shoot through my body. Every one of my nerve endings tingled with life. Once the fog in my mind cleared, I stood and tuned in to my surroundings. I tried to reach out with my mind, mentally begging for a sign of life in the woods around us.

"There are no animals here except for you, Sterling. I don't hear any bugs, birds not even a rabbit. They're all gone."

"Duh, I bet you flambéed everything within a two-mile radius. I have been around for a lot of years and I've never seen power like that!"

"Great, now I'm a bunny murderess." I hung my head in absolute despair, retching and heaving with the shame of what I had done. If I had performed a grounding ceremony, my magic would not have gotten so far out of control. "This is exactly why magic should never be used for personal gain." I wiped my mouth with the hem of my torn tank top.

"When the Council of Elders catches me, they will have my ass locked up forever. When I die, I'll go to Hell."

I wasn't whining, just being realistic. I had created one hell of a shit-storm and there was nowhere to hide. Hell, I couldn't even go anywhere. I had keys to a car that was melted below the pile of rubble that used to be my beautiful home.

"Shit, shit, and shit. What have I done?" I whispered.

* * * *

Sterling and I walked towards town. "Hopefully, no one in Salem Ridge knows what I did, yet. I'll go to the bank, get money out of our account and maybe Dawn will let me use their computer to order us some plane tickets. We'll go far away from here. We might be able to hide out long enough to come up with a better plan."

"I don't think you'll be going anywhere, Selena."

Roberta? Startled, I sent her flying with a wave of my hand. My crystal and ring turned black and I felt power building up inside of me again.

"Selena control it!" Sterling shouted.

"Yes Selena, control it." Roberta picked herself up and dusted off her behind with dramatic flair. Her wiry, red-orange hair stood out in angry tufts full of ash and dirt. "Is that any way to welcome a visitor?"

"Screw you, Roberta. Come one step closer and I will fry your slutty, demon ass."

"Tsk, tsk witch. Such a mouth. Do you kiss Shawn with that filthy hole of yours? What happened to sweet Selena? You have no idea who you're messing with and I must insist you calm the fuck down." She snarled.

"Oh, I think I know perfectly well just who and what you are. I command you to leave now, troll." I raised my hand again and Roberta raised hers in a mock surrender.

"I really wish you'd hear me out, Selena. Can't we just talk like adults? Is it really necessary to resort to theatrics and parlor tricks? Come now, you know you're no match for me."

I rolled my eyes and with a flick of my finger, sent her flying through the air once more. Roberta landed with a resounding thump in the pile of debris that used to be my apple grove. The woman truly had nerve!

"I told you to leave, Roberta. Staying here will get you killed. My mother sent stronger demons than you back to Hell and I will not hesitate to use my own powers to send *you* back burning with bells on. You and your *lover's* days are numbered."

My mother and I had created enough spells to send demons away. I'd watched her cast them out a few times. I'd have sent Shawn sooner if I hadn't been so stupid. Many filthy, ugly creatures fled into Hell just to escape my mother's wrath. Most of them, we never heard from again. Once in a while, we got a brave one who would come back for more, but my mother was a vehement demon-hunting witch. Almost as if she, herself, was possessed with the desire to eradicate them from the Earth. I never knew what drove her to become such an avid huntress, but I know she wouldn't rest until the demon she was after had been killed.

Sometimes, she would hunt them for days, stopping only when she absolutely needed to rest, eat or use the bathroom. One of the last hunts I remembered her speak of kept my mother busy for three weeks. The crafty demon was a shape-shifter who sucked the soul out of every body he hijacked. There were twenty-five funerals in one month. That's a lot, even for a town of paranormal and human inhabitants.

Roberta lifted herself off the ground with ease and landed a few feet from me. "Really? Where is your beloved mommy?" She laughed like a nasty old hen. "So, I see you finally know the truth?"

The bitch spoke in riddles. No wonder my gut told me to hate her when we met. She was fucking nuts!

"Fuck off, Roberta! Do not bring my mother into this! You know where my mother is, how dare you speak of her. I know way more than I ever wanted to know about you and your demon boy. Neither of you know anything about 'truth' so save your hot air for someone who gives a shit! You both sicken me. Maybe you should go running back to your puppet master and tell him I'm coming for him. You both know what I am, the heritage I come from and what I am capable of. Do not fuck with me." The words that flew out my mouth made me sound much calmer than I felt. I hoped I'd gotten my point across, but with an idiot of Roberta's magnitude, chances were, the conversation was far from over. The bitch just kept on pushing my buttons, almost as if she'd hoped I'd kill her and send her funky ass back to Hell.

"Puppet master? Ha! You have no idea. Shawn isn't the one in charge, Selena. He is a pathetic piece of shit. One might describe him as an end to a means." She shuffled her feet like a marionette dancer, skipping and shuffling without rhyme or reason.

What. The. Fuck? Every moment she appeared more and more insane.

"What are you talking about, Roberta? Never mind, I couldn't care less. Just go back to wherever you came from before I rip you apart and send your disgusting leftovers into the afterlife."

"You're just so cute when you're feisty." Again she laughed, scrunching up her face as though she were speaking to a child.

The woman's voice was like razors on metal. I wanted to rip her throat out and she stood before me running her mouth like she didn't have a care in the world. More of those homicidal urges pulsed through me, like voices whispering words of love, caressing me with their promises of desires fulfilled. I couldn't understand my recent urges to inflict suffering and pain, but I loved it!

"I can see why Shawn fell for someone like you, Selena. You're all cute and needy, but feisty when your feathers get ruffled. Such a turn-on for a man who needs his ego and other things stroked day and night. Don't you love the way he…"

"You know nothing about me, Roberta." I growled like some wild animal. She needed to shut the fuck up before I ripped her skinny lips off of her distorted, pig-like face!

We stood there glaring at each other and for the life of me I could not understand why Shawn had fallen into bed with this vile bitch! Roberta McManus was around five-foot-three and a little on the, ahem, chunky side. She resembled a matronly woman in every way possible, clear down to her sensible shoes. Roberta's eyes were pea green and the edges appeared to glow with bile yellow rings like a rabid raccoon. As far as her face went, I was truly in disbelief. I'm no beauty queen, but the woman was hideous. Oddly shaped with no cheekbone structure or even a chin! I could only imagine what that creature looked like when she went full-on demon troll! Strange as it was, I almost giggled at the imagery floating through my mind.

"Shouldn't you still be in Germany stroking his ego, Roberta? I'm sure he misses his little troll whore."

"Ouch. Kitty has claws, huh? But they'll need to be sharper if you hope to injure me. Your words are useless. You should shut up and listen once in a while, coward. Isn't that what you are? A little fucking coward? Too afraid to face the truth and now look where it's gotten you. Here with me." Clapping her hands, she bounced around like a cricket.

"I am so done with this conversation. We're leaving. C'mon Sterling."

As we turned to resume our walk, she shouted, "NO!"

"Excuse me? Do you really think you can boss me around? Fuck you, Roberta." I once again sent her flying. This time she slammed into a giant, old oak tree in the woods. The full force of my magic was ripping through me, begging me to keep going. Hurt her some more. Inflict pain, tear her apart. Shove my fist through her stinking face.

"Sterling, hide." I whispered and prepared for another round with the troll. I could feel and smell her coming. Her stench, much like a dead, rotten fish on the shore, had surrounded me.

"Please don't, Mistress? Let's just leave. Staying will only make things worse for us." Sterling pleaded and patted my leg with his soft paws.

"Be a good girl, Selena, stay and chat with me. I promise you'll want to hear this." Roberta slithered through the forest on her belly. Not yet in demon form, yet not quite human. She was fucking freaky! I'd forgotten how weird demons could be and how frightening their many forms could appear.

I summoned a binding spell and wrapped her in invisible threads of gold as she rose to her feet. "Speak, Roberta. You have one minute. What do you want?"

"Is this really necessary? After all, you're so much more powerful than little old me." She giggled and had the nerve to appear innocent, almost child-like. Her voice took on an angelic quality, sweet and deceiving at the same time.

"Fifty seconds, bitch. Talk or die."

"Oh well, if you insist on being such a stickler, I'll tell you."
She spoke in her librarian-ish voice, all prim and proper. "I want
your powers. And you're going to give them to me or I'll kill you."
Her face twisted into a grotesque version of her former self. Yeah,
she was ugly but this form was the shit nightmares were made of!

She smiled as she flexed her arms, breaking the threads of
gold as though they were made of nothing but air and sent me
flying through the air. I landed on what used to be my roof just
before she pounced on top of me. I rolled her over and grabbed
ahold of her red-orange hair, slamming her head against the green
metal roof, bashing her skull like a tiny piñata until I thought it'd
pop. Bam! Bam! Bam! I could feel her tiny, demon brain sloshing
around in her oversized head. Still, she laughed and rolled her
eyes, truly deranged beyond belief.

"I gave you a chance to leave, Roberta. You should have
listened." I hissed, squeezing her ugly face between my fists as I
shoved the back of her head onto the ridges of the metal sheeting.

I felt my eyes change as my powers shot white hot bolts of
electricity through me and into the sides of Roberta's head.
Momentarily it shut her filthy mouth and I took the opportunity to
punch her in the face, sending a spray of blood from her miniscule
lips and bulbous snout. She looked at me with a maniacal, serial
killer glare and before I could react, Roberta head-butted me,
knocking me on my ass. I cradled my throbbing head between my
hands just long enough to get my bearings before I launched
myself away from her to get on my feet.

"Wrong move, bitch." I wiped the slow trickle of blood from
my forehead before it got in my eyes and I noticed I should be
exhausted but I felt more awake than I'd ever been. Each time I hit
her, I felt invincible. With every drop of her blood, I became intent
on spilling more of it for her.

Growling like a wild animal, I soared through the air and
grabbed her by her bloody, tangled hair and threw her into the air
again. She reappeared in front of me almost instantly.

"Listen Selena, you're all alone. No one is here to help you
and I *will* destroy you. You're no match for me. You may as well
give up." Roberta stood a few feet from me, attempting to fluff her
matted hair.

"I'm not going to give you my powers, Roberta. In fact, they won't even be mine to give to anyone. The Council will be here to take them because of Shawn and you. This is all because of you!"

"Well, I do enjoy taking credit for such things, but this mess is your fault. Not mine. And when the Council of Elders gets here, they will put two and two together and you'll be charged with more than 'bunny murder'. Ironically, this crime scene looks just like what happened when your parents died. Oh, and you know that wolf friend of yours who lost his mother and brothers in a horrible 'hunting accident'? It also looked like this." She pointed all around us.

"What? What wolf friend? I don't have any 'wolf friends'. And of course this scene looks like the accident scene where my parents died, their house *exploded!*"

"Yes, it did. And you were the only survivor. Didn't you ever find that to be odd? The Council sure did. And now they will reopen that case. I wonder what conclusion they will come to. And don't play stupid, you know exactly what wolf I am talking about. Your 'soul-mate', the one with fur and fangs."

"You crazy bitch! You knew this would happen? *You killed my parents?*"

"Ding, ding, ding! You really are an idiot! Well, the truth, Selena, is Shawn killed them and made it look like *you* did it. I made you black-out during the weeks that followed so you'd have no memory of the events. You were so easy. Haven't you ever wondered why so many people abandoned you? They *know* your true nature, but they lack enough proof to 'throw you to the wolves', so to speak. I'm not surprised that it has taken you so long to catch up! You've always been a little slow on the uptake. No matter. The important thing is you're in a whole lot of trouble, girlie. Now what are we going to do about that?"

I launched myself at her and sent us both tumbling through the leaves and dirt. I smashed her face over and over again. When that wasn't enough to satisfy my desire, I shot more of my power into her skull, lighting the bitch up like a holiday tree. Volt after volt shot through her and still she laughed!

"Shit!" I launched myself off of her and landed on my feet a few yards away. Panting and soaked with rain and sweat, I stood there waiting for her next move. This was getting us nowhere. As soon as she pounced, I planned on slicing her in half. I was done playing games and I didn't have time for this redundant shit!

"Ha, ha, ha. You truly crack me up, Selena. We should do this more often."

Her hair stuck out in a jowl length mass of orange frizz and I had to suppress a laugh. She was truly disgusting and I couldn't wait to kill her. Unfortunately, she vanished and reappeared behind me. Sneaky bitch!

"I've had so much fun with you dear, but I really have to be going." She whispered in my ear. I spun around a second too late, sending a shot of sparks from my hand into empty space as she reappeared further away.

"You'll be having more visitors soon, coward. I'll be in touch. Until then, go find your wolf and tell him I'm coming for the rest of his family. Unless *you* think you can stop me, Selena. Take special care of that crystal. I'll be coming back for it." Swirls of vipers surrounded her, slithering in and out of her until she disappeared in a puff of smoke, leaving her laughter echoing through the canyon.

Was the entire town full of snake demons? What the hell had I been missing? I knew I was more than a fool and had no idea what to do. All I knew was Roberta was definitely more than a simple, easy-to-deal-with troll. She had seemed to suck the magic out of me and into her own body. My head was spinning with an insane amount of disbelief.

"What a crazy bitch."

Chapter Seven

It was still raining, but the downpour had slowed to a sprinkle. I scooped Sterling up in my arms and we headed towards town. Luckily, we didn't run into any more trouble before getting there. We had no neighbors up on our hill, and those who lived closer to town were already at work. Sometimes, I was very grateful for our seclusion. This was one of those times. At least no one had witnessed my meltdown or the sparring match with Roberta.

"Everything outside of our property appears to be unscathed, Selena. That's a good sign. The less people who know about the incident, the better. Thank the Goddess for the rain. If the fire had kept burning, the damage would have been much worse. And you would have had a lot of explaining to do."

"I think people are going to know something is wrong when I show up at the bank looking like this. I'm a mess!"

"Say nothing. Just go in and withdraw the money. If you need to use a spell on them, go ahead. It won't really matter at this point."

"True. Are you going in with me or are you waiting outside?"

"Outside. I'll hide by the back door."

I set him down on the sidewalk.

"Whistle for me when you are ready, Mistress."

"Love you, Sterling."

He winked as he scampered off, chasing a butterfly for show.

Thank the Goddess there weren't any other customers inside the bank. Dawn Jasper waved as I approached her window.

"Hi Selena. Haven't seen you in a while."

"Hi Dawn. I've been a bit, um, busy."

"I can see that. Are you okay? You seem…" I knew my disheveled appearance wouldn't go unnoticed.

"No worries, I've been working outside a lot. With the warmer than usual spring weather, I figured I would get a jump on the dead-heading and weed pulling. There is a ton of debris left over from last year. It's a never ending job."

"I can see that" she laughed. "So what can I do for you today?"

"I need to withdraw some money, please?"

"Sure. Just fill out this slip and I'll get you on your way."

When I handed it back to her, I saw the look of shock flitter across her face.

"Wow! You must be planning one heck of a shindig! It's for the wedding, right?"

"Um…yeah. Everyone wants their money today or no wedding. Florist, bakery, band and all of them say today is the deadline. And you know how temperamental the florist and bakery can be." I laughed.

"I sure do. They're a bunch of divas. Sit tight and I'll go get your money, sweetie." Amusement lit her eyes and she smiled as she walked into the vault. The amount of my withdrawal was too large to be kept at the counter. After the bank manager oversaw the withdrawal amount, Dawn returned to the counter with a green zippered money pouch.

Dawn counted it out for me, gave me a new balance receipt and said, "There you go. Good luck and best wishes." One of the town busy-bodies, Mrs. Bladdon, walked in and Dawn lowered her voice.

"Um…Selena, I know a lot of people have given you grief over your decisions after your parents died. And I know many of them don't like Shawn, but I'm not one of them. I'm here if you ever need anything. Okay? Don't listen to them, just be happy. I wish you all the best, sweetie."

"Thank you Dawn." Though I had tears in my eyes, they weren't tears of sadness. Having someone speak so kindly to me was something new, and right then, I needed it. I could only hope I'd get another chance to talk to her when my visit with the Council was over.

"See you later."

I walked out of the bank into the sunshine and whistled for my familiar. We walked through town quickly and managed to make it to a cute little store with minimal stares from the townspeople who were out and about.

Leaving Sterling outside again, I walked into Unique Ladies, a trendy and well, for lack of a better word, unique, store for women.

Their inventory varied, consisting of everything in retro style dishes and relics to modern day clothing and jewelry. The owner, Mrs. Bladdon, was still at the bank, so I knew I had a bit of time to pick out at least an outfit and a few necessities. I knew I could conjure up whatever I needed, even money, but I was trying to stay below the radar long enough to get Sterling to safety before they came for me. If I used any more magic, they'd hone in on my location and I had no idea who would end up with Sterling.

There were items on every available surface, so I did my best to scan the room quickly, hoping my eyes would land on something, anything I could or would wear. Sure the racks contained tons of pants, shirts and skirts but finding my size, however, turned out to be a difficult task. I picked out ten items and each one I tried on was too big, short, or ugly. I realized I had to lower my standards, a lot. Exasperated, I selected the only things I could tolerate wearing, at least until I was able to get to a store that offered more age-appropriate attire for me.

I chose and completed my purchases without one iota of drama unfolding. I was quite sure my outfit would cause enough drama of its own and exited the store with trepidation. When I stepped outside in my pedal pushers and polo shirt, the look on my cat's face caused my cheeks to color.

"Cute duds." Sterling winked just before falling on the ground in a fit of laughter.

To the non-paranormal passersby, Sterling appeared to be rolling on the sidewalk, perhaps scratching that one place he couldn't quite reach. But I knew what he was doing and my already bruised self-esteem couldn't take anymore. I pretended to ignore his antics and straightened my spine with indifference to the stares from the curious onlookers.

"Yeah, yeah, let's get a move on. You're causing a scene. We need to find a car and get to the airport. I couldn't ask Dawn to use her computer, I chickened out. So we will arrange our flight when we get to the Salem Ridge airfield office."

"Me? Causing a scene? Ha! Did you look in a mirror before you bought those clothes?" Again with the laughter, Sterling trotted beside me giggling.

"You're really enjoying this, aren't you?" I squinted my eyes against the sun as we walked under the different sized trees lining

Main Street and the beams of light that broke through in various spots.

"You're right, Selena. I'm sorry. You know how I feel about dogs, and I hate to bring this up, but I think we need to talk to the wolf."

"She lied. That's what demons do, Sterling. I don't know any wolf."

"You do. I smelled him on you yesterday."

"You smelled dog hair because of Janice, I told you that."

"Selena, wake up! Keith *is* your wolf."

"I think I'd know if Keith were a wolf. I've known his family my entire life."

He placed his paws on my leg, begging me with his eyes. "Fine. Just go see him. He will help us, whether he is a wolf or not. I know he will. He has to."

As we walked to Tooth & Nail, I was full of conflicting emotions. After the way I'd defended Shawn to Keith yesterday, I felt stupid and ashamed.

"Does Kelly think I killed her mom and brothers? Is that why she hates me? Could she believe I'm some evil, horrible person who would go around killing the people I know and love? What if I did kill them and I just don't remember?"

"You haven't killed anyone, Selena. Don't let that lying bitch, Roberta get to you. She's a demon. They lie. You said so yourself."

"Some of the things she said were true."

"You're no murderer. I've never been whammied or glamoured by you and I know what the truth is. I will tell the Council everything I know and they will listen to me." He did his best to calm my overactive mind, but I could only feign belief. My entire world had spun out of control.

"Sterling, I hope so. You're all I've got. I blew up whatever proof I had of Shawn and Roberta on my computer. I have nothing to show the elders and no one else on my side." I'd never felt so lost, confused and scared. I was sure the Council would fry me as soon as they had the opportunity. I'd go down in history as the witch the elders had to kill for the safety of man and paranormal kind. I was so fucked.

"I told you I will help and Keith will, too. We'll figure out something together. I promise." He rubbed against my leg in a reassuring and loving gesture, reminding me he wasn't just my cat. Sterling was so much more than that, he was my best friend and my better, often smarter, half.

"You're right. Let's do this."

Picking Sterling up, I held him in my arms as I pushed open the door to the pub. Once again, I was grateful to see there weren't many people inside at this early hour. Keith was just coming out of the back and our eyes met.

"Selena?" He rushed to set down a box of whiskey he was carrying. "Great Goddess! Are you alright?"

Immediately tears poured down my face. He was in front of me before I could sniffle. Keith ushered us to a table and eased me into the booth before he walked away. When he returned, he placed a bowl of cream in front of Sterling and glass of water in front of me.

"I...think...I need...something...a bit stronger than that." I tried to smile, but it only caused more tears to flow.

What the hell was wrong with me? Where had those tears come from? I didn't cry when I saw the photos of Shawn screwing Roberta, so why was I a ball of waterworks as soon as I'd set eyes on Keith? I'd lost my marbles.

"You're a mess! What happened?" His eyes were full of an emotion I couldn't decipher as he scanned me from head to toe. I couldn't tell if he was afraid or angry or both, but mentioning how horrible I looked didn't help. No wonder he was still single.

"Thanks, way to make a girl feel better, cowboy." I tried to offset the mood with some humor as I rolled my eyes and attempted a half-hearted smile, feigning offense at his comment.

"I didn't mean to upset you, but look at yourself. You're wearing peach pedal-pushers and a neon green polo shirt! Where'd those clothes come from, the Salem Ridge Golf Store? So not your usual style. Not to mention, your hair is standing on end and you have dirt all over your face. And why do you have dried blood in your hair?" He reached for my hand. "Please tell me what's going on?"

I didn't know what to say about the fact he knew what 'pedal-pushers' were. I'd store that away for a later date. And I hadn't even thought about my face and hair. Looking at Sterling, he confirmed with a little shrug what Keith had said. Great! I'd walked in carrying my cat while looking like a murderous street urchin! Yes, even at that moment, my shallow side reared its ugly head. I laid my head on the table and howled, crying like an injured hyena. I'm sure the few customers that were there were annoyed by my behavior and I didn't care. I just bawled and bawled.

"Okay, sit tight. I'll be right back." As if I really had a choice? I couldn't go out in public looking like this again. Where would I have gone anyways?

This time, he brought a bottle of Silver tequila and a glass of ice. Pouring me a very liberal shot, he said, "Drink."

I held the ice back with my left and hand and tipped the glass with my right, downing the shot like an old pro. After pouring me three more shots and watching as I sucked them down, Keith sat back with his arms crossed over his middle.

"Ready to talk now?"

What came out of my mouth was a story that began with Janice eating her poodle, quickly slurred into a jabbering mess of demons fucking, my cabin exploding, soul-mates and ending with me crying while I yelled, "I'm a bunny murderer!" Then I promptly collapsed with my head on the table. Yeah, I passed out, sitting there in my pedal-pushers.

* * * *

For the second time that day, I woke up with a pounding headache. I closed my eyes against the offensive lighting and groaned, "This is getting old."

"Afternoon, sunshine."

"What? Ah!" I looked up to see the most gorgeous eyes staring into mine. I closed my eyes and pulled myself into a sitting position as shards of glass pounded into my brain. Well, that's what it felt like. Truth of it was I was uninjured, but a bit hung-over.

"Easy there, Kitten."

"Oh Keith, it's just you."

"Yeah just me. Here, take these and drink this."

We were in his office and I was grateful for the privacy. I took a long swallow of the water he offered and then took the ibuprofen he handed to me.

"Thank you." I found I was full of shame as I remembered my fabulous bawl-baby outbreak and couldn't look at him again. So when he tipped my chin up with his fingers, my lip quivered and tears burned my eyes, threatening to pour out, I shrugged away. "I feel ridiculous for being such a blubbering fool. I'm, *um*...just gonna go now. Thank you for being so kind and I'm sorry I bothered you. It was a mistake to come here."

"No Selena. You're staying. It's my turn to talk and by the sound of things, you need to listen to all of it whether you want to or not."

His piercing blue eyes sent shivers of desire through me and I chastised my body for betraying my overwrought mind. I wasn't in the mood to be told what to do. Even if I needed the help and even if this handsome Cowboy Casanova was doing the telling. I was known to be obstinate to the end, but I knew I had no choice. I gave in. However, I wasn't happy about it.

"Fine, talk. But know this, nothing you will say is going to solve this mess."

I crossed my arms, jutting my chin as I stared at him with indifference. What about this man made my hackles rise so often and why couldn't I just appreciate his kindness when it was offered? Like I said, I'd lost my marbles.

Chapter Eight

He moved a leather chair over and placed it in front of me. We were eye-to-eye as he leaned forward, placing his elbows on his knees.

"I know you're upset, but you have to remain calm and listen, okay? There are so many things I'm about to say that will sound crazy, but trust me, you need to hear them."

His serious tone scared me and though I'd just had a glass of water, my mouth was dry and my throat felt tight.

"I'll try but I don't think I can handle many more surprises." I giggled. Yeah, giggled. I've always had this habit of almost laughing and crying simultaneously whenever something made me nervous. Not the most endearing little quirk. When I was younger some people said it made me seem a bit crazy, but it was one annoying habit I'd never outgrown.

"Too bad, Kitten. What I'm about to say will shock you but it may just save your life. So, toughen up and get ready."

"What could you possibly know? You haven't spoken to me for years. Up until yesterday, I had no idea if you were alive or dead." I huffed. How did Keith think he knew anything about me?

"While you were asleep, Sterling filled us in on what happened."

Keith was nuts. Yep, that's why I never ended up with him. He was certifiable. Did he honestly expect me to believe my cat talked to *him*? I shook my head, another bubble of laughter escaped and I stared at the crazy man across from me.

"What do you mean, 'he filled us in'? And who is 'us'?" My already raw emotions were teetering on the edge of another bout of panic and I swore I must be dreaming. I felt like Alice in Wonderland, but I didn't remember passing any rabbit holes on my way to Tooth & Nail. Hysteria threatened to pour out of me as realization dawned on me.

"There's no way you could have heard him unless you're..." the words died in my throat as Keith nodded.

"A lot of what Roberta said to you was true. I'm a shifter. A werewolf to be exact, and so is my entire family. Well, what's left of it."

I jumped up and backed away from him, swaying with shock. "Shit! How? I mean, when? What?"

"Please sit down before you fall down."

"I think I will stay over here, thank you." He couldn't possibly think I'd believe him, could he? I pinched myself and even tried pulling a handful of my hair, assuring myself I was indeed wide awake.

"Fine, stand. Just stop hurting yourself. Believe me, you're awake." Keith held his arm out, offering his hand, but I remained a few feet away with my arms crossed over my middle. With a sigh, he continued, "Remember when Dad sent me to Tennessee?"

I nodded. "How could I forget? I was heartbroken." Oops, I said that out loud. I sank into a chair as I cursed the filter between my brain and my mouth for again taking a leave of absence.

"Heartbroken, really? Well, well, well." His eyes danced with amusement as he grinned and I swore he blushed a bit. "Never mind that, back to what I was saying, for now."

It was my turn to blush and I sat back down. Inside I was a mess and my emotions were going in a million different directions. He found it amusing I'd had a crush on him and all I wanted to do was to run like a scared rabbit. I didn't need his condescending smiles, placating me like a schoolgirl.

"The truth is I was going to be sent to Tennessee anyway. It was planned even before my mom and brothers were killed. All of the males in our pack go to specific camps until we can control the change. The date of my trip was moved up due to the timing of their deaths and the fact my change was happening at the same time as Kelly's.

"Going to Tennessee was the way to ensure that the people I loved could be kept safe, safe from me and from whoever might be gunning for my sister and dad. And it gave my dad time to clear his head, handle pack business and investigate what was happening. It's easier to take care of a female wolf when she begins her transformation. Though, they become a bit more emotional, okay, a lot more emotional, the females don't go as primal as the males and they don't attack anything that breathes like we males do."

He continued as I sat there silently, afraid to move. Keith was serious. How had I missed this? Why had no one told me?

"Breathe, Selena. Kelly completed her transition with the help of my aunt. She came to town during Kelly's senior year of high school. That's why she stopped hanging out with you. She was a mess. Imagine PMS only a million times worse with an appetite for blood and destruction. She was such a bitch. Literally." He laughed.

A hint of a smile escaped my lips, but confusion kept me silent. How could I have never known Keith was from a family, a pack, of werewolves? I swore the room was spinning. Don't get me wrong, I know Salem Ridge has a mixture of humans and paranormals, but it's often hard to distinguish them from each other unless they tell you or unless you've known each other your entire lives. Even then, apparently that wasn't a guarantee you could really know someone. It's not like everyone roamed the streets in the form of wolves, vampires and demons. Our town was a haven, but most people still enjoyed their privacy and anonymity.

Our townspeople held their heritage close to their hearts. That's why so many hated me for abandoning mine. None of the others were ashamed or afraid of what they truly were. To them, the relinquishing of my powers was like a slap in the face. I was beginning to understand why Kelly hated me so much. She had been going through a terrible ordeal and I'd only been thinking of myself. No wonder we'd drifted apart. I was just as much to blame as she was, if not more.

"She doesn't hate you. Maybe she doesn't understand why you stopped practicing your craft, but she does not hate you."

"What?" How did he know what I'd been thinking? The grin on his face cleared up that issue. Great, he could read my mind too. "Aren't a woman's thoughts supposed to be sacred or something? Hello? Invasion of privacy? And why didn't you tell me? We grew up together, Keith! What the hell?"

"I wouldn't be able to read your thoughts if we weren't destined to be soul-mates. But that's another subject for later." He smiled as my jaw dropped wide open, almost hitting the floor. "And even though we live in Salem Ridge, it isn't exactly normal to walk around shouting that we're werewolves. We needed to keep it quiet. My family was safe for a very long time because no one knew what we were."

"Stop. Stop it right now, Keith Jacobs! You're talking in riddles. First you hear my cat, and then you inform me I'm in danger. Now we're soul-mates? You just told me you're a werewolf! And how can we be soul-mates? Wouldn't that be like bestiality or something? What the hell is going on? Is this a joke?"

I could feel a wave of energy pulse through me as my emotional state grew out of control. It was too much to handle. My instincts were screaming for me to lash out. So many lies and betrayals, and all of them were from the people I'd loved most in the world. I didn't want to hurt Keith, but I wasn't sure if I could stop it.

Selena, breathe and just listen to my voice. Let it ground you. Take a deep breath. I'm not going to hurt you. Look at me.

He sounded so far away, as if he was in a tunnel. When I looked at him, I could see my glowing eyes reflected in his. Oh no! Not again!

His hands were suddenly on my upper arms with his fingers digging in and the pain was delicious, and only caused my energy to expand, filling me. *Selena, listen and breathe. It's okay.*

His lips weren't moving! He was *in* my head! Oh my Goddess! I jumped up and away from him again. As soon as I broke our contact, all of the light bulbs in the room exploded and shards of glass rained down upon us. There were so many fragments littering the floor it looked like it was made of diamonds.

"Shit! Are you okay, Selena?" He yanked me into his arms and crushed me to his solid chest.

"Mmm?" I mumbled into his chest. I pushed myself away from him a bit and asked, "Are *you* okay? My powers are kinda' out of control."

"I'm fine. Don't worry about me. If I had been injured, I would heal at a faster rate anyway. It is you I am worried about. Especially your timing. Why couldn't you have waited until daylight to blow my light bulbs to smithereens?"

"Ha-ha. You're such a comedian."

Smiling, he brushed bits of glass off of my head and arms and grabbed a large white candle off of his bookshelf and struck a match to light it. The amber glow lit up the darkened room sufficiently for us to grab the trash can, dustpan and broom in the corner. We silently worked side-by-side, for what felt like hours until we'd checked every possible surface for stray slivers to dispose of.

"About your ability to heal faster, today, after my fight with Roberta, I was able to heal quite quickly, too. I never knew I'd be able to do that. And except for these damn headaches and the ability to blow shit up, I'm just fabulous."

In his eyes I saw kindness and in my mind, I heard him say, *I'm sorry.*

"Don't worry about it. It isn't your fault and stay out of my head!"

"If you could hear me, then why didn't you calm down?"

"Seriously? You scared the shit out of me! Warn a girl next time, Keith. Jeez! You don't just pop into someone's mind and think it will have a soothing effect."

"Okay, you got it. Next time I'll say, 'Hey, Selena I'm gonna hop on in now. Do you mind?'" Rolling his eyes to the ceiling, he continued, "That should come in real handy if we're ever in danger. I'll just ask before I tell you how to save your ass."

"Just full of sarcasm, aren't you, wolf boy?"

"You asked for it. So, you believe me?"

"How could I not? We live in Salem Ridge. I'm still pissed, though. And what makes you think you'll have to save my ass? I'm not exactly a weakling, ya know?"

I glared at him, as I prepared to launch another verbal attack.

He raised his hands in surrender. "Okay. You're right. But it was the only way I could think of to make you understand quickly."

"Understand what, exactly? I already know I can blow shit up. That's one thing I don't need assistance with, believe me." Sighing, I shook my head and thought of yet another mess I had created.

"We're meant to be together, Selena. We always have been."

"I think I need another drink, a big one."

"No more drinking until we're done talking."

"You're not my boss, Keith. Werewolf or not, you will not tell me what to do." We both stood there, arms crossed, and at a stalemate. He wasn't going to budge. No drink for me.

"Fine, would you please have your sister bring my cat in here? I don't really feel comfortable leaving him alone with her."

"Sterling is perfectly safe. You have my word."

What he failed to understand about me was that no one came between Sterling and me. He was and always would be my first concern. Regardless of the fact that I'd not picked up on Shawn's demon mojo, if I felt Sterling was in danger, I wanted him by my side. I would move the Earth to keep him safe and there wasn't a dog alive that would stop me. His words failed to reassure me and I wasn't about to back down.

"Well, excuse me if I don't exactly trust your word. Seeing as how your family has lied to me for years, I'm not really ready to trust any of you right now." Glaring at him, I raised my chin in defiance, showing him I was not going to be deterred so easily.

He laughed. "You've always been so damn cute when you're angry, Kitten. But one of these days, that stubbornness will get you into trouble."

"I'm not your kitten."

"You are," he smirked. "And you're a hot little kitten when you're all fired up and glowing."

"No. I'm. Not." Full of petulance, I stomped my foot on the floor. Yeah, I know, real mature. Why couldn't I get my shit together around this guy? One minute I'd been an evil sorceress who made things explode, the next I acted like a spoiled three-year-old.

"Okay, okay. Ha-ha-ha. I believe you. Now please stop pouting and sit back down."

"And if I don't want to?" Again like a child? It was so infuriating!

He stood where he was not budging. "Then, no Sterling."

"Two can play this game. I want my familiar now, Keith or I will walk out of here and we'll never speak again."

"Fine." He relented, clearly not happy about being beaten by a girl. Did I just think that? A girl? God!

"But I warn you, Kelly won't be happy about it. She's been enjoying the last few hours as a cat-sitter. Stay here. I'll go get some new bulbs and grab Sterling for you."

Raising my eyebrows, I remained ramrod straight until he left in a shroud of silence.

"This is just what I need. An entire fucking family of cocky-assed werewolves and they may even be a bit crazy," I whispered, when I was sure he was far enough out of ear, er, mind-intruding distance. I twirled my long blonde hair through my fingers while details of the past twenty-four hours flew through my mind like pissed-off bumble bees.

What the hell? Witches and werewolves could not be soul-mates. It wasn't possible. Was it? I knew I needed more answers and wished my mother was there. She'd know what to do. My head felt like it was about to implode and all I wanted to do was sleep. "Please let all of this is a very bad dream or just some fucked-up universal joke."

I sat down on the desk chair and stared out the windows for what felt like an eternity. "Goddess, I'm so confused." Sure, I'd always been attracted to Keith. Hell, when I was ten years old, I'd even planned our wedding. In fact, I had kept the book full of ideas and details. Check that. I'd had the book until it was burned to a crisp that morning along with everything else I owned. I never once envisioned marrying a wolf!

The realization that Roberta was right pissed me off! What did that bitch really hope to gain? She had powers of her own so why did she need mine? So many questions and I needed answers.

"It's time I calmed down and listened for once." My life and the lives of many others apparently depended on it.

* * * *

Keith opened the door with one hand and carried a very defiant, very pissed off Sterling with the other. Neither of them looked very happy about being together.

"You know, just because I played fetch with your sister and let her rub dog scent all over me, it doesn't mean you can put your paws all over me, Fido!" Sterling squirmed and wiggled trying to escape Keith's strong grip.

That was my Sterling, always good for a giggle. Seeing him filled me with warmth. Some things never changed and in that moment I was so grateful for that small miracle.

"Hi buddy." Sterling launched himself out of Keith's arms, landing on the leather sofa. He climbed up on the back cushions and began to bathe.

"Yuck! I taste like mutt! This smell better come off or I will take it out of your hide, Wolf man."

I walked over and rubbed Sterling's chin. "Sterling, be nice. Kelly and Keith have been very hospitable and I think it's time we both show a little appreciation. Okay?"

"Whatever." He grumbled and turned his back to me.

"You wanted me to bring us here. What's changed?"

"What's changed? I'll tell you what's changed! Kelly brought dog toys outside for me. Dog toys! Do I look like a dog? I thought these people, these animals were supposed to be smart? Let me just say that I would never recommend them to work as service dogs. These nincompoops would bring pogo sticks to people who are in wheelchairs!" He yelled in high-pitched, hysterical tones and I'd never seen him this way. Not once had Sterling ever been so mean, at least not to anyone's face. Clearly, the stress of our situation had been getting to him, too.

"Sterling! Stop it! You apologize right now!"

"They should apologize to me!"

"Fine, we will all apologize and make nice. We don't have time for any of us to have attitudes."

After a round of mumbled apologies, I let out a huge breath. The day had been so exhausting and it'd only just begun. What would it be like living in the same house as these two, all of us, three completely different beings? What? Same house? What was I thinking?

"Keith? If you're still willing to talk to me, I'm ready to listen."

He smiled with perfectly even, white teeth and I held back the...*my, what big teeth you have* comment that floated through my mind. Yay me! I guessed the filter was at least half-assed working for now anyways.

Keith just shook his head and smiled even more. Apparently, my filter didn't keep him from hearing my joke. Giving him a mock glare, I flopped down on the sofa beside Sterling.

"Alright, I told Kelly to run home and get something. We're all out of light bulbs, so for now we will use candles. We've closed the bar for tonight, so we shouldn't be interrupted."

"Closed? Because of me? But you can't. Everyone will be upset and in this economy you can't afford to lose their business. Besides, where will all of them go? For most of them, this place is their nightly ritual."

"Don't worry about our financial situation and they'll live. There is too much to explain and way too much to do. We have no idea how much time we have, so let's get to it. Help me light these candles, okay?"

In a few moments, the entire room glowed with gorgeous amber lighting, casting dancing shadows all around us. It was soothing and I found myself relaxing in the small but comfortable space.

Kelly knocked and poked her nose in.

"Hey Kell, c'mon in."

She shut the door behind her and handed Keith what looked like a very old book. I was immediately drawn to its soft-looking, brown, leather exterior. As I watched Keith set it down on his desk, my first instinct was to pounce on it and grab it. It called to me as if it was my very own.

"In time, Selena." Keith's voice snapped me out of my dreamlike state.

"What just happened?"

"In a few minutes I will tell you. Okay?" He patted my hand, but showed no emotion. His face was grim and serious. My eyes, huge round orbs, shot back and forth between the two Jacobs siblings, asking a hundred questions as I silently pleaded for answers.

"Selena?" Kelly spoke up and drew my immediate attention to her. "Keith and I will help you however we can. Just trust us, okay?" She sat beside me and held my hands in hers. Tears pooled in her eyes as she attempted a smile. Though there was kindness and caring written all over her face, I knew I was in for more so-called truth.

Shit. It was not going to be good.

Chapter Nine

"Y'all are scaring me. What's going on?"

"Well, you already know what we are and now it's time for you to know what you really are."

"What I *really* am? I'm a witch and I already know that."

"I think what Keith meant to say was that it's time for you to know what *else* you are." Kelly soothed.

"What else I am? Are you insane? I'd think I would know if I were something else." My mouth went dry and my palms were sweaty. These people had to be nutty. My eyes again darted back and forth between the two of them, hoping they'd admit they were joking. Nope. Serious as heart-attacks, they were.

"When your mother died, Elena's spirit paid us a visit. She had so many things to tell you, but she never had the chance. And when you quit practicing magic, she believed there would be no getting through to you. You closed the door that would've allowed her in." Kelly's voice was soothing, though her words tore at my heart. I longed to see my mother again, to hear her again, and I'd have given anything to have just a few moments with her.

"What did she say?" My lips trembled as I spoke and Kelly tilted her head a bit and took a deep breath.

"Well, you already know how she felt about your relationship with Shawn. He was always around and she knew you wouldn't listen to any talk of the craft. Your mom knew all of these recent events would happen. Roberta, Shawn, all of it, was a constant worry for your mother. However, Elena had hoped you would be away from Shawn sooner. She had no way of stopping any of this after she died and honestly, she couldn't have done so when she was alive. All she could do was give us some of the information and hope you'd find your way through it all with minimal damage. After you became engaged, it made it difficult to bring up the subject in conversation and she stopped trying. The events were already set in motion."

"You practically became a hermit, Selena, and we thought it was too late" Kelly whispered.

"Too late for what?"

"Selena, your mom knew Shawn was a demon. She even told you what she knew. Don't you remember?"

"Yes, but I figured she was just upset that I was growing up. I never dreamed she meant a *real* demon. You know how mothers can be. I thought she was acting like an overprotective mom, watching out for her only daughter. Back then, I was annoyed. Now, I wish I had been more mature and listened."

"I'm sure being upset was part of her reaction about Shawn" Keith mumbled. "But you have to know, the things she said came from her heart and the knowledge she gained over the years from her own experiences."

"She also knew Roberta, who's the reason, well *most* of the reason that all of this has been happening."

"Duh. She's a home-wrecking whore. But like I've said, I'm over Shawn and their relationship is none of my business. I'll be happy when I can get this damn ring off and go on with my life. I just want them to leave me alone."

"I'm afraid that can't and won't happen until you kill *her*." Kelly said.

"Gladly."

"We're serious" Keith interjected. "And you may not feel the same after you hear the rest of what we are about to tell you."

If the looks on their faces were anything to go by, it still never would have been enough to gauge the impact of what they were about to say. Bracing myself for the worst, I had no idea their words would change my world forever.

"Selena, Roberta is your half-sister."

"What? You're bat-shit crazy, Keith!" I shot out of my seat and laughed until my sides felt like they were exploding. Tears poured down my cheeks and I couldn't look at the two of them without bursting into another fit of hysteria. They sat motionless, not speaking and after a few moments I realized my antics weren't getting one giggle out them.

"Okay, joke's over. You've had your fun. I admit you really had me for a second there. You both look serious enough to be telling the truth but I see this is 'poke fun at Selena day'."

"Selena!" Sterling piped up from his position in the peanut-gallery.

"It's true" Kelly said. "Your father, your real father was sent away when you were just a baby. Once your mom realized what a monster he was, she called the Council on him. His name is Samuel and he's a demon."

Kelly avoided looking at me for as long as she could. Keith reached for my hand and I slapped it away.

"What? Don't touch me! You're both fucking nuts! You're lying. Why are you saying these horrible things to me? I thought you were going to help me? Help me what? Get a first class room in the loony bin? Don't worry, I will tell them to keep the doors unlocked and beds ready for the both of you. You need serious help!"

"Selena."

"No! Shut up! I've had enough of this truth bullshit! I swear everyone has gone insane and I will not stay here and listen to another word!" They didn't say a word. They let me rant until I couldn't think of another thing to yell or scream at them. Keith and Kelly sat there and took every horrible thing I said to them without batting an eyelash. When I ran out of steam, Kelly patted the chair beside her.

They were serious. The looks on their faces told me they weren't lying. Was that because they believed what they'd said or because what they said was true? Why did I feel like I was at a funeral, a funeral I'd had no idea was mine? When I'd taken enough deep breaths and calmed down, I shot questions at them like crazy.

"What about my dad, the dad I have known as my father for my entire life? That was a lie? How can I be a demon, half-demon, quarter-demon, what the-fuck-ever? How can any of this be possible? I don't understand!"

"When your mom first met Samuel, he tricked her much like Shawn tricked you. She fell in love with him just like you fell in love with Shawn. One night, not long after you were born, your mom used this book and overheard him whispering to you in another language." He touched the magnificent leather-bound tome. "She found he had been talking to you in demon-speak. He called you 'his future, his wicked princess'. A few days later, she turned him in to the Elders but it didn't break the spell on you even though he was sent away."

"Spell? What kind of spell?"

Kelly sighed "He wove a spell around you that would show itself when you turned twenty-five. All it needed was a catalyst, a traumatic event to make it come alive. He believed that you would come into your demon powers and turn your back completely on the craft. If the events could force you to step over that line of good and evil, he believed you would come to Hell and save him from his prison. Last night, you came very close to crossing that line. In the process, it awakened all of your demonic abilities. Combined with your craft abilities, you have the power to free not only Samuel, but as many demons as you please."

"Why would I do that?"

"I'm not saying you will. This is what Samuel believes. Once you return to Hell, he will have won."

"Return? How can I return when I have never been there?"

You were created in Hell, Selena. He captured the lost spirits of others in his legion, Trillmor, and created you, a new spirit. Once he spilled his seed into your mother, you took form."

"So, I'm evil? I'm really a demon? Is that why Shawn wanted me, because I'm a nasty, beast from Hell waiting to wreak havoc on Earth? I'm some kind of fucked-up demonic hybrid?"

"No. You're not *evil*, per se. But you could be if you don't learn to control your powers. All of them. The choice will always be yours and yours alone."

What could I say? In just a few moments, I'd found out my entire life had been a lie? The last twenty-four hours had been a complete nightmare. A real, living nightmare and I was the psychotic starlet.

"What about Roberta?"

"Your father created her after the Council of Elders and Elena banished him to Hell again. He thought Roberta might be strong enough to release him, but that hasn't worked so far. Let's just say Roberta is a lab rat gone wrong. He can't control her." Kelly said.

"Great. So they sent Shawn to trick me into a relationship that was a lie, pulled my strings like I'm their personal puppet? They hoped I'd go all 'wicked' when I realized Shawn had cheated on me, correct? They thought *that* would be enough to push me over the edge?"

"Sort of. When you found out about his betrayal, they assumed you would go ballistic."

"And you did," Keith said. "You used your magic for revenge and that is going to bring the Council to town. Once they bind you, Roberta believes she can use your crystal to free Samuel."

"I'm sure Samuel was hoping that you would have been angry and far gone enough to kill someone with your powers, cutting Roberta out of the equation. If an innocent had died, you'd have crossed that line and evil would have taken control of you. You would free Samuel and together destroy the Council of Elders. There would be no need for Samuel, Roberta and Shawn to steal your powers because you'd be one of them."

"*They* murdered my mom and dad. Roberta admitted it. She said it was part of the plan. Something about me using fire last night and now I've made myself look guilty of their murders."

"Yes, they killed your parents and you played right into their hands by destroying your home. I ran out there to look around. It's bad, Selena. It looks just like your parents' house looked after the supposed 'accident'."

The reality of the situation hit me with such ferocity, yet I felt numb. I could never track all of the questions and thoughts running around my mind. I could only be glad that I wasn't feeling energy pulse through me. For some reason, I felt stable amidst all of the mental chaos.

"If all of this is true, then I *need* to be locked up and powerless. I shouldn't be allowed to roam free. Call the Council and let them take me so I can't hurt anyone."

"That isn't an option, Selena. Besides, there's more."

"You've got to be fucking kidding me. *More?*"

"Yes. They didn't just frame you for two murders, your parents' murders. They framed you for five. My family wasn't killed in a hunting accident, the cabin blew up."

My jaw hit the floor. *Ohmigoddess,* no!

"Your mom and brothers? You have to know I didn't kill them!" I looked at them both, begging them with my eyes to believe me.

"Of course we know that. But right after your mom and dad died, you went catatonic. You wouldn't speak to anyone in town for weeks. Every day, you stayed locked inside your cabin with

Shawn. The entire town, including me at one time, has thought *you* killed them and escaped justice. That's the real reason they, all of us, have avoided you and treated you horribly." Kelly hung her head, ashamed.

"I thought you were all mad simply because I quit using magic. Now, you're telling me everyone thinks I'm a murdering harlot? Including both of you?"

"The fact you stopped magic has been part of it, yes. But they feel you killed Elena and Joseph in a fit of rage because they didn't approve of your decision to quit magic or your decision to be with Shawn. They feel you turned your back on the town and everything Salem Ridge stands for. Peace, equality, harmony. They stay away because they are afraid of you. That's also why they stay quiet. As for us, Keith and I eventually realized that none of it was your fault. But, in the beginning, you have to admit, it looked really bad. And now that you've blown up your own home, it will be harder to convince them of your innocence."

I sat with my head bowed in my hands. "Do they know I'm a demon too?"

"Part demon," Kelly soothed. "You're not *all* evil. And no, they don't know, yet."

"What if I really killed them? Maybe I went on some crazy demon-rampage and blocked it out?"

"You didn't." Keith's voice was tender and I knew he believed every word he said, but I didn't.

"How can you know that?" I whispered.

"I can read your thoughts, remember? We're connected, we always have been."

"What if Shawn whammied my memories? What if Roberta pulled some mind-zapping trick and I wandered around blowing people to smithereens?" Tears trickled down my face as hopelessness set in.

"Why me?" I asked.

"Why not? You're strong, smart and capable of handling this, and we believe in you. Besides, at least we have each other." Kelly countered.

We all took a much needed break and made dinner in the pub's kitchen. It seemed strange to be working side by side in almost total silence. In light of what had been revealed to me and what was about to happen, we found a bit of comfort in the menial task of cooking. It was the only normal thing about that entire day and I wished for it to never end. I didn't think I could handle what the universe was bringing to me. All I wanted to do was sit somewhere and cry. However, inside, my mind battled with my bruised and beaten heart, saying *you've never been a quitter. You won't start now.* Sure I was. I had quit magic, quit a lot of things. What in the world was I going to do?

As we sat down to eat, I could feel many unanswered questions bubbling inside of me. I knew Keith and Kelly also needed answers and I wished I could be the one provide them. The situation weighed heavy on all of us while we ate in silence. But I knew there were still many things to be said.

"I'm so sorry."

"For what?" Kelly asked.

"For all of this. Your family was murdered because of me. Even if I didn't do it, it was because of my powers. I'm truly sorry."

"Not just because of you. Our mother was next in line to be an Elder. She helped your mom banish Samuel to Trillmor."

"See?" Keith asked.

"See what?" I sniffled, wiping tears away as I waited for his reply.

"You're not evil. If you were, you wouldn't care about any of that, anyone else or anything except or your own selfish desires. You'd be rejoicing instead of apologizing. It will be okay, Kitten." He squeezed my hand and fresh tears poured once more.

When did I turn into such a crybaby? This was really damned annoying. I never used to cry!

"After dinner, we'll talk more. For now, just try to relax. Okay, Selena?"

I gave Kelly a quick nod that I hoped was convincing.

We cleared away our dishes, placing them in the sink to be washed later. I wiped down the table we had used and swept the crumbs up off of the floor. Keith offered to escort Sterling outside to attend to his kitty needs, but Sterling assured him he could use the toilet like everyone else. Keith looked at me, shocked, and I nodded.

"He even puts the lid back down and flushes. Just make you sure you turn the light on for him."

Kelly and I brewed a pot of fresh coffee for the long night ahead of us, while the males busied themselves elsewhere.

"You okay?"

"Sure. I mean…no. But I have to be, don't I?"

"Right. I'm sorry for the way I've treated you the last few years. None of us knew how to handle any of this. Yesterday, when you heard Keith and me arguing at the bar, he wanted to tell you the truth then. Maybe if we had…"

"Don't. It isn't your fault. You couldn't have known I'd go all 'Queen of Pyros' so soon. No one knew except Roberta."

"I still feel horrible about it. Keith knew Shawn was with Roberta. When he told me, I should've said something. I haven't exactly behaved like a best friend, have I? I wish I could've, would've, told you. And for the record, I've missed you." She enveloped me in a huge hug. I held onto her for dear life, as we wept together for our families, for ourselves.

* * * *

When Keith and Sterling returned, we carried a tray of coffee, creamer and sugar into the office and sat down. Sterling climbed back up on his perch on the back of the sofa, declaring it his spot.

"Okay. So I guess I need to figure out what I'm going to do. I have to stop them."

"What did Roberta say? What were her exact words?" Keith took a huge sip of coffee, grimaced and added another packet of creamer.

"You still use only creamer?" He nodded and I smiled at yet another thing that hadn't changed in all of these years. "Basically, she wants my powers and she told me to tell you that she is coming for you, coming for your family."

"How does she plan on getting your powers? When?"

I don't know. The Council will be here to take me to trial and my powers will be bound inside my crystal. Roberta believes Shawn and she can get them from me once they are bound inside my crystal."

"Maybe that's the only way they can take them?" Kelly asked.

I shook my head. "My mother said they cannot be released until a witch's sentence is up. So, once my powers are bound, only the Elders can free them. If a witch tries to break the crystal, she is immediately banished to Summerland's dungeons. There she will stay until she dies. As far as I know, no one else, nothing else, can get their hands on my powers."

"Roberta thinks you'll just hand her your crystal? Based on what? I bet she plans on busting it open and you'll be locked away while she frees your father. She's going to take the credit and be daddy's little number one demon."

"He's *not* my father." They both stared at me.

"Okay. He *is*. Technically. But you know what I meant. Can't we just call him Samuel? Please? The father I knew is dead. Samuel will never be my dad."

"Sure, Selena. You're right. We'll call him Samuel." Keith poured himself another cup of coffee and added another ten creamer packets.

"Good. So now, we need to know why she wants to kill the rest of your family. Sorry, but they already got your mom and brothers so what would be the point in killing the rest of you?"

"To keep you away from Keith" Kelly said.

"I don't get it."

"Yeah. I don't understand that part either. But that bitch is going to pay for everything she has done. I'll enjoy ripping her to shreds. Let her try to come after us." Kelly glared. "I'm ready for her." As she examined her nails, the look on her face was truly bone-chilling.

With a shiver, I turned to Keith. "What does your dad say about all of this?"

"Not much. Besides, he is out on a hunting trip with a few of the other packs. I can't even reach him by phone to warn him. They're somewhere in the Appalachians."

"What about that book? Maybe it has the answers we need?" Besides, I still felt that book reaching out, beckoning to me. I needed to get my hot little hands on it again.

"We'll see. For now, we all need to get some rest. I have some blankets and pillows in the closet and that sofa is a sleeper. This building is far safer than any other I know of. I've spent many nights here sacked out on that couch after doing inventory and nothing bad has ever happened." He offered me a smile as he held out blankets and pillows to Kelly and me.

I said nothing, but inside, I didn't think we would ever be safe again.

Chapter Ten

Kelly and I shared the sofa bed and Keith was curled up in a sleeping bag on the floor. I waited until I was sure the others were asleep and eased myself out of bed. Tiptoeing with my ears attuned for the slightest movement or change in breathing, I crept to the desk and spotted the one thing I knew would have the answers I craved.

The book lay exactly where Keith had left it. As I ran my hand over the well-worn, brown leather I could feel it speaking to my soul. There were runes inscribed on the cover and I traced them in a clockwise motion with my fingertip as I whispered the name of each one. In the center connecting every symbol, there was an aquamarine encrusted pentagram. When I touched the beautiful gem, it glowed and felt warm to my touch.

A gentle breeze swirled around me and the book opened itself. Inside the cover, names were inscribed in gold lettering. Names of every witch before me who had possessed this book since its beginning. Before my very eyes, an amber glow lit the page and I watched as my own name magically appeared in the same fancy script as the others. "I knew this was meant for me. Thank you, Mom." I whispered.

Sterling stirred and stretched. Quietly he crept over to the desk and hopped up to sit beside me. "What is it, Selena?"

"It's everything." And it was *mine*. I could not explain the sense of power and possessiveness I felt for this book. I only knew I couldn't close it. It spoke to me, promising gifts of knowledge and power I had never fathomed.

I grabbed the book and held it like a treasure as we tiptoed around Keith's still form. Once out in the hallway, I shut the door as quietly as I could. Sterling and I sat in the booth farthest from the office and away from any windows.

"How did you never see this book, Sterling? You were around Mom for years."

He shrugged his little gray shoulders and gave no sign he knew anything about the beautiful book. "Your mom was always talking in her sleep about 'the book'. I thought she was just dreaming."

"It's so gorgeous. Do you smell it? The pages smell like Summerland. Fresh and inviting. If one could put hope into a book, this is what it would look and smell like."

"Sweetie, that smell is mildew and age. Achew!"

"Drama queen."

"Touché."

"There has to be a spell in here that will help me get this ring off."

"Let's hope so. I'd like to avoid another run in with Roberta the troll, if at all possible."

The book gave details on the long line of witches I came from. My family lineage dated from before the Salem Witch Trials. No, we don't live in *that* Salem. Our ancestors thought it would be best to move far, far away from the hysteria. For the travelers, finding the mountain upon which Salem Ridge was eventually settled and nestled into, was pure luck and convenience. With the Ohio River running through it, it offered plenty of farming, shipping and trade opportunities. Besides, most people, humans, that is, would never assume real witches lived in Salem Ridge. Back then, everyone was focused on settling along the eastern seaboard, eradicating the people they believed to be witches and as many Native Americans as they could. It was a horrible, horrible time in history full of ignorance and murder. Those who survived, headed West.

They were too busy to notice or care when the real witches left Salem and moved. There were still many deaths, crops failed, and livestock perished, but they continued to seek out the 'sinners who caused the wrath of God to punish all of them'. The townspeople blamed everyone else for the naturally occurring phenomena that comes with settling in a new land. To put it as nicely as I can, the people in Salem were nuts. Plain and simple, they were all bat-shit crazy.

To most people, the Salem Witch Trials are nothing more than folklore used by 'honorable men' to scare the sinful onto the 'right' path. If I had been there, I would've asked them, "Do you believe any god would want only people scared into believing in him or her?" I didn't think so, but you can't change stupidity.

Nevertheless, their actions made it easier for our families to hide in plain sight.

In the years following my family's arrival, more and more of the so-called different and evil folks came here for refuge. What started out as a hiding place, grew and prospered. It even turned into a very popular tourist destination and comfortable village. Truth be told, it's the only spot used for the Underground Railroad that no one ever detected. Our town has helped many escape different types of demons, even the human kind.

"So much I never knew about our town is in here, Sterling. It's amazing!"

I read on and on. There was even information about my great, great, great, great, great-aunt Elizabeth. She was one of the very first to step foot here with her husband, a Shawnee Indian named Chief Red Eye. After most of the members of his village in Pennsylvania were slaughtered, he traveled as far west as he could. Meeting my aunt in Ohio saved his life, for he had no idea of the slaughter taking place along the coast. They were inseparable from their very first meeting. Together, they settled in Indiana, founding Salem Ridge and welcoming everyone who wandered into town.

"She's given credit for creating this haven. Apparently she and the chief protected a lot of people until the day they died. I wonder if they're together in Summerland?"

"I believe it. Your family has always been good."

"Until Mom met Samuel, right?" How did she even meet him? Was he a resident? Did he seek her out? Still so many questions paraded through my mind.

"Read on, Selena. I want to hear more."

"Here we go. Samuel's real name is Samell. He is one of the guardians of the Trillmor legion. Oh, he is really bad, Sterling! Look at his picture!"

"Whoa! Look at those hooves! He is one ugly beast! Glad you look like your mom." He snickered and patted me on the shoulder with one soft gray paw.

"Thanks."

"Selena, it says he is also a shifter. This picture is only one of his many forms. He can look like anyone or anything once he is freed from his prison."

"That must be how he fooled Mom for so long. We can't let him escape again. He killed thousands of people by himself. Now, he has an entire legion of demons at his beck and call. If he gets out, the world will literally go to hell in a handbasket!"

As we read on, I realized a few things. One, Roberta didn't know half as much as she thought she did. Two, I needed to keep the ring on until I killed her and made sure Samell stayed in his prison. Though I hated the demonic tracking device, I was going to use it to my full advantage.

"It says here, the Council will definitely bind my powers to my crystal. Good. I need them to."

"Are you nuts? How will you fight Roberta, Shawn and Samell?"

"Maybe I won't have to."

"Selena?"

"Don't worry, Sterling. It will be okay. I promise. Now, I just need a plan."

"Preferably one that doesn't include you turning into a fire-throwing serial killer."

"Thanks for the vote of confidence."

He shrugged.

"According to this, the enforcers for the Elders could be here anytime. We'd better get some sleep. Who knows how long the trial will last."

Sterling shivered, sending tiny, gray hairs everywhere.

"Selena?"

"Yeah?"

He stood there staring at me, silent—a very rare thing for him to be. "Cat got your tongue?" I joked.

"Ha-ha," he sighed. "I just want you to know, I um, really *didn't* mind playing with Kelly today. She's not so bad for a mongrel. And Keith doesn't really stink that much. I don't mind being around them."

I knew in his own way he was saying he'd be okay if he had to stay with them for an extended period of time. Though I appreciated his attempt at easing my mind should anything happen, I hoped more than anything, he wouldn't have to live with them, without me. I didn't plan on leaving him on his own, but it was good to know I had friends who would care for him if...

"Remember, I can read your thoughts, Mistress. This plan of yours? Please be careful. I've really enjoyed those gourmet cat treats you've always bought for me. I wouldn't want to have to be without them."

"I love you, too Fuzzy Nuts." I kissed the top of his head and I swear I saw a tear fall from his beautiful emerald eye as he hopped down and ran to the hallway. We both climbed back into bed, but neither of us slept much, too nervous for what the day ahead would bring. I lay there thinking about what I would do, who I was and what it meant, and I knew I needed help. Lots of help.

In my ear, I heard my mother whisper, "You can do this Selena. I believe in you."

* * * *

The next morning, I stood at Keith's office window while the sun shone as if the universe didn't have a care in the world. Maybe it didn't. But all I could wonder was what the day would bring. I must've been far away in my own thoughts because I never heard him walk up behind me and I jumped a bit when he rubbed his hands up and down my arms.

"Sleep well?"

"You bet." I turned around to face him and smiled.

"You didn't sleep at all, did you?"

My sideways glance spoke volumes.

"Are you okay?" he asked.

"Sure."

"How 'bout we get some breakfast, then we'll check out that book together. I tried to open it but it wouldn't budge. Maybe you can figure it out."

I turned away from him. "I already opened it, Keith. There wasn't anything helpful in it."

"Already opened it? How? And there was nothing? A huge, super-secret book and there wasn't anything helpful inside?"

"It spoke to me. Well, it lit up actually and opened on its own when I touched it. But it was simply a book documenting the history of my family, nothing more."

"Oh. Sorry. We hoped there would be more to it."

"Yeah, me too."

"Well," he ran his hand through his gorgeous hair and sighed, "what do we do now?"

"The only thing we can do. Have breakfast and wait for the enforcers to get here."

I patted his cheek and walked out of the room pretending to be much calmer than I was and hoped the butterflies of apprehension I had felt all morning would leave so I could eat.

We worked together to make a huge buffet. There were pancakes, eggs, bacon, sausage and everything in between.

"This is really nice," Kelly said. "All of us together." She placed a platter of tuna and chicken mixed with scrambled eggs on the table for Sterling. Kelly rubbed his chin and smooched him on the head. The whole scene brought tears to my eyes.

"Yeah, it is nice." I sighed and dabbed my eyes with a napkin.

"Look, Selena I know you're nervous but we'll be right there with you. Everything will be fine. You'll see." She squeezed my hand and smiled. Her blue eyes betrayed her. She was just as scared as I was, if not more.

After washing our dishes and completing our 'busy work', Kelly announced it was time to open Tooth & Nail for the day. She shifted from foot to foot nervously and looked at me full of apologies.

"It's okay. I don't want to cause you to lose any more business. What can I do to help?"

"Oh, nothing. All I have to do is unlock the door and turn on the beer signs. Folks will start to trickle in as soon as they see the lights go on."

"Damn! The other lights! I'm so sorry."

"I forgot, Selena. We'll be fine, no worries. It will be daylight for a while, so we'll be able to see." She tied a red apron around her waist and finished setting up glasses for the day.

"Really, I'd like to fix the lights. After all, I broke them. How about I run over to Hanner's Hardware and grab some bulbs? While I'm there, I will see if they have some clothes for me to wear today. I refuse to go back into Unique Ladies with Mrs. Bladdon working."

"I don't blame you. That woman is mean." She mock-snarled, raising her newly painted nails like claws.

"I'll just grab my money and I'll be back in a jiffy."

"Okay. I'll let Keith know. Thanks Selena."

"It's the least I can do, I blew all of the bulbs." I plastered on a happy face and bounced out the door, pretending to be the confident woman I truly wanted to be.

Word must've spread like wildfire through town. The people on the sidewalk gave me a wide berth and every time I waved, they either turned away or ducked. How ridiculous could they be? Did they think I would launch fire balls at their heads on Main Street? Wow!

I was both shocked and amused by their ignorance. Groups of busybodies whispered to each other as I walked by.

"Wicked."

"Shameful."

"Harlot."

And the last one nearly knocked me over. Our town psychic, Mrs. Woods, muttered, "Half-breed."

My head turned so fast, I was surprised it didn't snap off. Of course *she* would know. The fact that she hadn't told me, lit a small fire of irritation within me. I saw the look of fear on the little old woman's face as my eyes lit up. She turned and practically ran in the opposite direction, leaving her friends to stand there with their jaws hanging down.

Holding my head high, I walked into Hanner's Hardware & General Store and selected a shopping cart. After I found the light bulbs, I loaded up twenty boxes of them. There were so many lights at Tooth & Nail and I wanted extras in case I blew my top again.

I wandered over to the work-clothes section and spotted quite a few items I could tolerate wearing. Thank the Goddess Hanner's carried something close to my size. Kelly and I used to share clothing, but she'd put on a lot more muscle over the years than I had. Now I knew why. After all, one couldn't be puny *and* a werewolf. It just wasn't possible. I laughed to myself when I thought how silly she would look all furry with gangly pre-teen legs and spindly arms.

I grabbed a light blue t-shirt with the store logo on it and selected a pair of off-brand jeans. I knew they'd be a bit short, thanks to legs that start at my neck, but I could roll them up like 1960's capris. On a shelf in the front of the store, I found plain, white canvas tennis shoes for three dollars a pair. Again, they had something close enough to my size. I walked over to the so-called beauty section and grabbed the necessary toiletries before remembering to add a few more essentials to my enormous haul of loot.

"Too bad their panty selection is butt-ugly," I whispered. "But, I will take what I can get for now."

As I approached the check-out counter, I swore I saw Phyllis cringe. Her poppy-painted lips were pinched into a grimace and her brow was so tightly furrowed birds could've perched on the wrinkles it contained. She rang up my purchases and spoke only when they were totaled.

"One-ten-fifty-seven." She clipped, her eyes never once landing upon my face. Instead, she stared off at a seemingly more interesting spot on the far wall behind me.

I sighed and took out one-twenty and handed her the money with a smile.

Phyllis handed me the change, "Nine-forty-three." Not even a thank you or have a nice day.

I asked if I could use the restroom. "No. It's out of order." She avoided my eyes, so I knew she was lying.

"Oh, okay."

I realized there was no way I would be able to carry everything and said "I'll need to borrow the cart. I walked here and it's too much to carry back."

Phyllis Hanner looked down and said "I'm sorry. That's not allowed. The cart stays here."

"But Phyllis, please? These bulbs are for Tooth & Nail."

She patted at her blue-tinted hair "I'm sorry but you should have bought only what you could carry. It isn't *my* problem."

"Look, Phyllis I promise to bring it right back."

The sixty-ish woman busied herself with straightening stacks of brown paper bags. "I told you no. Please leave."

"How can you be like this? My family built this town and you were friends with my parents!" I was shocked and dismayed by yet another ignorant person's behavior and I wasn't going to take anymore.

She came out from behind the counter, lowered her glasses on her nose and whispered, "That was a very long time ago. Your parents are dead, a fact you and everyone else in town are very much aware of. Now, please leave." Her rheumy eyes bore into mine with hatred.

I could feel rage building up inside of me again. *Zap her!* My mind whispered. *You know you want to.* I knew I had to control the demon side of me and Phyllis hadn't made it easy for me.

"Phyllis, what exactly is your problem with me? Can't you just be a damn adult and explain why you and everyone else seem to find me so repulsive?"

"I don't owe you an explanation. Your actions speak volumes and we all know about the things you've done. Selena, you need to leave."

"I will not. Not until I get some straight answers. I've had it with you and everyone else treating me like garbage. I didn't do anything to any of you!"

The last bit came out much like a growl.

She closed her eyes shook her head as if it the action would make me disappear. "Please just go. No one wants you here. I don't want any trouble."

Excuse me? Did she say what I thought she said? How could grown people act like immature, junior-high schoolers? Evasive, ignorant bitch! Whatever!

"Fine. But I am taking the damn cart with me. You'll get it back when I feel like returning it." I planned on pushing the freaking cart right down the middle of Main Street. Hell, I might even sing and dance on my way back to Tooth & Nail.

It took a shitload of strength to push that damn wobble-wheeled piece of shit to the supposed automatic door. The wheels fought me every step of the way, making it feel like I was stuck in quicksand, sinking with every step. I hated carts! When I reached the door, I remembered it too, was out-of-service, just like the restroom, so I had to open it by hand. After I had one side open, I held it in place with my ass and pulled the cart forward. Everything was going great until I ran over my toes. "Shit!"

All I needed was to look like a fool and give these bitches more to talk about. "So much for a kick-ass, 'Mae West exit'." I looked more like a stupid comedy skit on that late night Saturday show.

Shoving it the rest of the way through, the handle bar plowed into my ribs. "What the fuck!" I pushed it with all of my strength and proceeded to stand there kicking the crap out of the worthless piece of fuck cart. Yes, tons of people were watching, but maybe they'd think I had gone completely nuts and leave me alone for good. I just didn't care anymore!

By the time I arrived back at Tooth & Nail, I was grouchy, sore and sweaty. I grabbed a few bags of bulbs and after I'd composed myself, sauntered through the wooden door as if I didn't have a care in the world and placed them on the bar top.

"Thanks, Selena."

"There's more. I'll be back."

Three trips later, I was exhausted and smelled disgusting. I told her Sterling and I were leaving. There wasn't any reason for them to be stuck with me or my drama. If we stayed, they'd just be in more danger. Besides, I needed some time alone to think.

"Leaving? Why?"

"I'm going over to the Upton House to rent us a room for the night. I need a shower and some time to get my mind straight for this trial."

"Keith will be back in a few minutes. He can take you out to our house." She smiled.

"No, Kelly. You guys have done way too much for me as it is. Besides, I need some time to myself before the Council gets here."

"Well, it isn't any inconvenience. When will you be back?"

"In a while or at the latest, tomorrow morning."

"All right. I'll let Keith know."

"See you soon."

I put my cat in the cart's basket and gave him a ride. Sterling and I took the cart back to Hanner's and parked it outside the store. I waved when Phyllis peered at me over her glasses. She visibly shivered and turned away. I scooped Sterling up in my arms and set him on the sidewalk so he could walk.

"That was fun! We need one of those!"

"You want a shopping cart? Great. Well, it does fit us. After all, we're officially homeless."

"For now, Mistress. But we'll be okay. Keith and Kelly want us to move in with them." I couldn't believe my ears! When had they discussed this?

"What?" I squawked.

"Yep, let's talk as we walk. I can't wait to get on a comfy, king-sized bed. Do you think they'll turn the bed down for us? Fluff our pillows and give me a bedtime treat, maybe?"

"I doubt it, Sterling. When did Keith say they want us to move in?"

"I overheard them say as soon as possible. He'll probably be mad we're staying at a hotel tonight. I think he was getting their house ready for us."

Sterling was chipper and he practically bounced while we walked. However, carrying the brown paper sack full of my meager belongings was only increasing my own irritation.

"I really need an overnight bag."

"For what? We don't have much, yet. Besides, Hanner's has them, you should've bought one while you were there."

"But we will have more to carry as soon as I can shop at a real store. I've got money and carrying it in this bank pouch is liable to get us mugged. Even if Hanner's did have them, I wouldn't have bought one from them if it was on clearance for a dollar! They can keep their garbage."

"Mugged? Here?" He dropped and rolled on the ground laughing. "Oh you're funny, Mistress!"

"I try. So glad I could entertain you, fuzz-butt." I curtsied and almost dropped my torn paper bag. Growling in frustration, I walked faster.

"What happened at Hanner's?"

"Never mind."

"Oh, more small town crazies?"

"Something like that."

"There it is, Selena. I can practically smell the goose down pillows!" He pounced on up the sidewalk and I could hear his purrs, though I was about ten feet behind him. With a cat that happy, it was hard not to be just as excited as he was.

"Let's hope they will rent us a room."

"Paws crossed. But if they give you any shit, we can always go back to the bar with Keith and Kelly." He smiled.

He had developed a potty mouth and wanted to stay with the Jacobs pack? What the fuck was wrong with my cat?

Chapter Eleven

Upton House rose before us like a temple. Situated on a hill on the western side of town, it was one of the most gorgeous, historic buildings in Salem Ridge. Building began in 1710 and was halted by lack of funds. In 1834 the Upton family spent sixty-two thousand dollars trying to finish it. Jonathon Upton died of tuberculosis before it could be completed.

Years later, an investor by the name of Thomas Fisher found the original blueprints and attacked the task feverishly. Thanks to the enormous amount of help from the townspeople, within a few months the fourth floor and its majestic towers were completed. The monolith mirrored Mr. Upton's original plans in every detail. To this day, the original blueprints, now framed in exquisite cherry frames, hang in the Great Room for all to see. If someone had built it to Mr. Upton's same standards, beginning to end without stopping, in our present day and age, it would've cost sixty-two million. Chances were, it never would've been built or finished.

"I'll never tire of looking at this beautiful place. Can you *feel* it, Sterling? The entire inn is pulsing with energy."

"I feel it, Selena. Are you okay?"

"Never better. Why?"

"Your crystal, it's um…glowing again," he whispered.

I looked down and to my surprise, he was right. "At least it's not black, right?" I laughed and didn't give the glowing pendulum another thought.

"Good point. Let's get inside, okay?" I didn't think about Sterling's sudden nervousness or what it meant. All I wanted was a shower and a few moments to myself. Living alone for years, I was used to having my own space. I loved my friends, the Jacobs, but every girl needs time on her own.

"Sure. My stomach is flipping a bit, but let's go. It's probably just nerves."

We walked in and approached Mr. Fisher's desk. "Hello, Mr. Fisher. I'd like to rent a room for the day."

"Well, I'm afraid we're all booked up, Miss Barnes."

"Really? There were no cars out front. Where's everyone hiding?"

Mr. Fisher's face turned a sickening shade of pink as he fumbled for excuses. His eyes darted side-to-side and everywhere else to avoid looking me in the eyes. There was even a pile of invisible dust that suddenly needed his attention. I watched unamused as he made a show of wiping it away. There was a lot of that 'pretend she isn't there' stuff going around and I wasn't backing down.

"Look Mr. Fisher, I have plenty of money to spare and I know you could use it, especially in these hard economic times. Is it wise to turn away a paying customer? Any paying customer? I simply need a room in which I can rest and take a shower. Please?"

"I already told you..."

"*Please* Mr. Fisher, please?" I whispered. My throat tightened and I knew tears wouldn't be too far away from falling. I just needed someone to give me a break. "Just twenty-four hours?"

He mulled it around in his mind for a minute and I silently begged the Goddess to convince him that I meant him no harm.

"Fine, all I have is the Honeymoon Suite. Four-hundred and seventy-nine dollars. Cash only. If there are any damages, I will call the police, the Council, and your fiancé."

"My fiancé? Well..."

"Like I said *no damages*. Cash only."

"That's fine." I counted out the five-hundred and told him to keep the change.

He laid the key on the desk, avoiding any chance of coming into contact with me. My evilness might've rubbed off on him. Ironic thing was, the people of the town had treated me far more cruelly than I ever would've treated them. I signed the receipt "Thank you so much."

"Room 218." And with that, Sterling and I were dismissed.

I carried Sterling as we made our way up the grand staircase. Wine-colored carpet now covered the antique steps and the stained glass windows cast colors of every shade across each one. It was like walking into a kaleidoscope. Though I savored every step of the way, all I could think of was a nice, hot shower.

We arrived at our room, silent and weary. I placed Sterling on the mahogany floor as I fumbled with the room key. No electronic cards for the Upton House. They still used real locks and long, skinny keys for every room. Another of the many things I loved about the home away from home. Each of its many irregularities as compared to today's modern age only added to the originality and nostalgia of the gorgeous house. Everyone felt as if they had stepped back in time, even if for only a moment. The way history was combined with a sparing few modern amenities was amazing.

"Here we go buddy, home sweet home. For a night anyways."

"Oh Goddess, look at this place!"

Sterling launched himself across the hardwood floor and landed on the plush, king-sized bed. His entire body, except for his long tail vanished beneath the pile of down-filled pillows. The cherry bed frame seemed to encase a giant wine and white colored marshmallow with gold trimmings. It was so decadent. I hadn't seen a bed that large or ornate in a very long time and I didn't blame him for his enthusiasm. It took every ounce of control I possessed not to run across the room and jump on it like a teenager at a slumber party. However, I refused to touch it until I'd had a shower. Sterling purred and stretched, and then he burrowed deeper under the stack of white pillows. I couldn't even see a whisker, he was truly in kitty heaven. I had to admit, it was nice seeing him acting like his old self again, if only for a little while.

Placing my brown, paper luggage on the dining table, I stepped out of the ridiculous, neon green flip-flops and reveled in the feel of the chocolate-colored dining room carpet. It was gorgeous to look at, but the feel of it was pure ecstasy. I loved the hardwood floors I'd had installed piece by piece in our now demolished cabin, but right then I was in love with the cushy, soft fabric that seemed to massage every inch of my feet. The floor alone pushed some of my stress away.

"Ohhh, I could walk on this forever."

"Mistress?" Sterling slithered out from under the mountain of pillows and cooed. "Can we get a bed like this?" He rolled over and over, rubbing his chin on the rich textured fabrics and purred louder than I'd ever heard him purr before.

"You bet. Anything you want. As soon as all of this is over, I'll buy everything you love and more. Even a new kitty condo if you want one."

"I don't care about the condo. Just get me this bed." With dramatic flair, he stood on his hind legs and flopped backwards and flapped his arms and legs as if he was making snow angels. That cat was something else! According to what my mother had told me his age was when we got him, Sterling would be fifty years old if he were human. Yet, there were times when his larger than life personality and desire to be carefree, made him seem like a footloose, fancy free teenager. Those were some of the best moments I'd ever had with my familiar.

"Okay, I'm hopping in the shower and then we'll order something to eat."

"Take your time, Selena. I'll be right here, catching up on my beauty sleep, blissful and snoozing." He winked and rolled around some more.

Goddess knew he needed sleep. He'd had a rough few days. He could sleep for hours on a good day if he chose to and good days had been in short supply as of late. At the least, I hoped not to bother him for the next half an hour or so.

I padded into the bathroom and located the light switch. The chandelier cast an amber glow that brought out the little flecks of gold in the natural pattern of the marble flooring and counter-space. The white and gold slabs adorned every surface from the floor to the vanity tops. Combined with the rich, brown paint on the walls, the bathroom reeked of opulence.

In the center of the room was a giant real copper tub encased in four foot marble walls, with steps leading into the tub and out. The separate shower was big enough for four people and its glass doors opened in three different places. Inside there were ten, yes, ten, shower heads pointing in every direction. I turned the knobs and the biggest spout above the shower poured like rain from its large round head, reminding me of those commercials for the honeymoon getaways on television where people laughed and showered together. In our room, however, I didn't have to worry about getting sand out of places sand should never be in and that in itself was a blessing.

"This is amazing." I ran my hand over the copper faucets, lost in their sleek and smooth feel. I missed my cabin and its stick built hand-picked amenities, but this room was pure decadence and I could see myself staying there for longer than one night, if the fates allowed.

I chose to try out the shower and promised myself a long soak in the tub later. I just needed to get clean. Turning on the knobs, I undressed as the water warmed up and filled the shower stall with a lavender scented steam. "Wow, pure relaxation from the get-go. Who knew there was a way to scent the water! I am truly in awe! These folks didn't mess around."

I placed my ugly peach and neon green clothing in the trash bin. I planned to burn them later. "Good riddance, pedal-pushers." I shivered.

Opening the glass shower door, I was immediately enveloped in the swirling steam and I spun in circles as I tried out every angle of the multiple shower heads. Being washed from every angle with little effort was an orgasm-inducing experience. I felt like I would melt into a puddle from the euphoria.

"This must be why there is a built in marble bench in here." I sat down and let the water pour around me as I closed my eyes and floated on a lavender-scented cloud of afterglow. The water streamed over me like satin ribbons and I moaned in ecstasy as my worries drifted away on the steam that poured out over the top of the shower walls and door.

"What an amazing invention. I wish I could stay here forever."

I must've dozed off while I sat there and it felt like a dream when I was awakened by a voice in my ear.

"Enjoying yourself, Cupcake?"

"Ah!" I tried to jump up, but to no avail. He had me pinned and the floor was too slippery for me to gain any footing. In front of me, mere inches from my face, Shawn stood in all of his demonic glory.

His forked tongue slithered out of his snarling lips and licked up the side of my face. I felt bile rise in my throat as he trailed his claws down the side of my neck. "Let go of me, asshole!"

"Shh. Now, now, is that any way to speak to your fiancé?" He laughed. "We wouldn't want to wake your familiar, now would we? I'd be forced to silence him."

"You wouldn't!"

"Really? You've already killed him once. That leaves eight more lives, correct? Believe me, I would enjoy watching him die over and over again. How you can love something as ugly as that walking fur-ball is beyond my comprehension."

"Have you ever looked in a mirror? You're a nasty beast!"

"A beast you fell in love with, no less, and I've never heard you complain before." He appraised me with yellow, beady eyes as he tilted his head side to side. "I've always loved your tight little body. I'll enjoy tearing into you. Now that you no longer smell like mutt, I bet you'll taste divine."

Ugh. He flicked his tongue out, wiggling it in front of my face and I wanted to rip it out of his scaly face. Rage was pulsing through me and I didn't know whether to embrace it and let it fill me with power or tamp it down to keep me from getting into more trouble. What was I supposed to do? No matter how I struggled, I couldn't escape his claws. With every movement, they dug into me deeper, angering me more and more.

"Let go of me, dammit!"

He pulled me to my feet and pinned me against the wall with one hairy thigh between my legs. I looked down and saw his hooves also had talon-like claws and my mind spun with fear as nausea filled me. I had never seen a demon this hideous and I'd certainly never fought one that large on my own. What the hell was I going to do?

"How nice of you to get us the Honeymoon Suite" he hissed. "But isn't it a bit too soon? The wedding isn't for a few weeks. Do you think your dear ole daddy will show up? Maybe he'll even walk you down the aisle and hand you over to me? Roberta will even stand in as your maid of honor. Wouldn't that be divine?" The demonic asshole had the nerve to wiggle his eyebrows as he pondered that plan.

"Fuck you and your troll-whore! There isn't going to be any wedding! And what about my father? You killed him before you could even get to know him, remember?" I'd be damned before I'd let him know how much I knew about Samell, or Samuel, as he was known to most people.

My breath was ragged and shallow as he shoved his chest against mine. If he pressed any harder, I'd become one with the marble wall. The pain was insane but I wouldn't let him know that. I knew he'd enjoy every suffering moment as he crushed me, breaking one rib at a time and as they drove into my organs one by one, and he'd count each heartbeat until my last.

"That ring says something entirely different. You're *mine,*" he growled. "And you will be until I no longer have a use for you. As for your father, you killed him. Remember?" He mimicked and goaded, pushing me closer to the edge of losing it.

"Really? Roberta says you killed him, Shawn."

"You're lying. She would never betray me like that. Besides, Roberta is still in Germany. You know nothing!"

He had no idea I knew Samell was my father or that I'd spoken to Roberta. Which meant he also had no idea I knew I was part demon. I tucked that bit of information away for now and took the opportunity to slam my forehead against his. It hurt like hell, but it stunned him long enough for me to escape his grasp.

Just as I reached one of the shower door handles, it exploded outward. I fell hard, and my face bounced on the glass coated marble floor. I rolled over as he stomped his way out of the shower. "Uh-oh. Cupcake has a boo-boo. Let me kiss it and make it better." He grabbed me by the hair without even leaning down. His arms were elongated and scaly on one side and covered in hair underneath. *What the fuck?*

I really should have studied up on demons last night. I was smack dab in the middle of a deep shit situation and I had no idea how to get out of it. My powers, good or evil were my only chance. There was no time to make a moral decision. It was live or die and if I died at his hands, he'd steal my powers before I could even blink.

He perched atop the marble steps of the tub and stood over me. "What do you want, Shawn? Why are you here wasting my time when you could be fucking your troll and making little ass-faced demon babies?"

He laughed a deep guttural cackle. "You know what I want. You're mine. Did you think I would let you run off and shack up with Jacobs? You will never be with that mongrel and I will kill you myself if I have to, just to keep you away from him. I have a wonderful future planned for us, Selena. It's about time you accepted that fact and started acting like a proper wife!"

"Why do you care? You have Roberta. Soon you'll have my powers. What more could you gain from keeping Keith and me apart?"

I swore steam rolled out of his huge, pointed ears. He slammed his fisted paw on the copper tub, caving in the one side. There went any hope of a luxurious bath later.

"I have no idea why I ever agreed to this plan. You are such a stupid, little bitch! We cannot *allow* you to mate with him, you idiot. And as long as I am around, it will not happen!"

"We'll see about that! You're disgusting and now that I know the truth, I will *never* be with you. I'm going to send you back to Hell with the rest of your sick friends."

"Sick? You want to talk about *sick?* Do you have any idea how much it disgusted me to put up with your incessant whining and complaining about your parents? And your lack of friends made you a pathetic, frigid bitch. I had hoped that ring would have loosened you up some, but no! The past four years have been pure torture and for what? Just to please…"

"Please who? What the hell are you talking about?" Samell of course, but he wouldn't say that. He believed they still had leverage with their secret.

Ever the conceited bastard, Shawn turned around to admire himself in the vanity mirror and I took the opportunity to slam his face into it. He never saw it coming. With a flick of my hand I rammed him into the broken glass until green ooze poured from his ugly face. I was disgusted by the grotesque scene, but the urge to fillet the nasty fuck didn't ebb.

"I fucking hate you!"

"Feeling's mutual, sweetie! So many nights, I wanted to gut you like a pig and wallow in your entrails. Don't look so disappointed, Cupcake. That day *will* come."

As he wiped his face with a paw, I noticed his constantly changing form. For some reason he couldn't control what shape he would be next. As horns grew from his head, I sent out a binding spell and he was tied to the floor by vines.

"It's bad enough that I have had to deal with this shit-storm you created, Shawn. Now, I have to pay the damages cost for this beautiful room because of you and that pisses me off."

"Oh, poor baby has to pay damages," he sing-songed.

I slapped him from across the room. He laughed and licked his lips, enjoying the violence.

"You'll never get away, Selena. We have eyes everywhere. After the Council binds your powers, you *will* surrender them and become my wife."

"Over my dead body. Why do you want my powers anyways? I'm sure they are nothing compared to yours, great demon," I taunted.

He narrowed his eyes and examined me, "I've always loved how naïve you are. You've made all of this so easy. Just a weak little girl and so effortlessly molded. Like my own personal poppet. Tell me, Selena, do you regret surrendering your powers? Do you wish you had told me the truth years ago? I cannot believe how dumb you thought I was. I've known about you since your birth, you wench!"

I couldn't take much more, I knew my eyes were glowing and this hotel room was not the place to blow sky high. "Shut up, demon! *I'm warning you!"*

"Oh? And what will you do, witch? Curse me with warts? Turn me into a toad? Please! We both know you're no match for me."

His condescending attitude, once attractive, coming across as self-assured and resilient, was more sickening than anything else. Why did Roberta and Shawn think they were so almighty? If they'd known what I was all along, they had to know I could annihilate them with little effort. What was with all of the constant taunts and jabs?

"If I'm merely a witch, why do you need my powers, Demon Boy?"

He shut up, knowing he was on the verge of saying too much.

"Tell me the truth or I'll kill you."

I could see his thoughts warring with each other as he tried to decide. In the end, he merely said, "You'll never kill me, witch. You can't. You need me."

"Ya' know? You are one ugly full of yourself, sonofabitch! Did Roberta piece you together from spare demon parts she had lying around? You're more of a mutt than Keith and his family could ever be. One minute, asshole. Speak or die."

His fury was growing, yet he said nothing. His anger was palpable as it pulsed through the floor and surrounded me. He couldn't stand anyone telling him the truth. Shawn believed he was god-like, all powerful and hot. His ego was too big to handle anyone hitting him with words of disgust. I whipped the energy inside of me into an enormous frenzy and produced a ball of green and brown tinted lightning between my hands. I poised it above my head as I counted down the seconds. "Ten...nine...eight...seven..."

He remained silent. By the time I got to six, I was over it and threw the lightning at him, hitting him in the chest.

"Do you have any idea how much vengeance I have rolling through me, demon? Tricking me with your lies was one thing, a mistake I could forgive. But killing my parents?" I created another ball of energy and it slammed into his head. "That was unforgivable. The *witch* you see before you is far more than you know. If I have to hunt you and your nasty, vile friends down for the rest of my life I will. I won't rest until all of you are back in Hell. Imprisoned or dead, it makes no difference to me. I have nothing left to lose. Tell them I'm coming for them!"

I threw a bolt of electricity at him and he vanished before it reached him. I collapsed on the floor as his voice rang out "See you in Hell, witch."

Chapter Twelve

"Selena," Sterling whispered as he tapped on the bathroom door. "Are you alright?"

"Yeah, I'm fine. I just slipped on the wet floor. I'll be out in a minute."

"I must've been whammied. I heard yelling but I couldn't link with your thoughts. Did something happen?"

"No, no. Everything is fine. I was bitching to myself for being such a klutz."

"Okay. Please be more careful."

"You bet." There was no reason to freak Sterling out more than he already was. Besides, I knew more trouble was on the way and he'd have a lot more to deal with.

"Mistress?"

"Yeah?"

"I don't want to be a jerk, but I can smell your new soap and it's horrendous. My advice is to throw it out."

"You're right. I'll throw the soap away."

I gazed around at the mess we'd made of the once beautiful bathroom and sighed. "I may as well fix it. I'm already in deep shit with the Council."

Grounding myself, I called on the elements and my Goddess as I envisioned golden beams of light tethering me to the earth. A blinding white light washed over me, its comforting presence filling me with an inner peace. When I felt calm enough, I imagined the entire room put back in order. The towels were hung, the floor was dry, the mirror was back in one piece and all was right again. My cuts were sealed and I wished the dried blood away. After I thanked the Goddess and Mother Earth and released the leftover magic to return to the universe, I felt refreshed and ready to face the next obstacles, dressing and finding food.

"So it is, so shall it be."

Walking into the dining area, I retrieved my clothes and put them on in the bedroom. There was no point in hanging onto modesty when Shawn and his whore could pop in at any given moment if they chose to do so.

"There. That's better." Did you decide what you want from room service, Sterling?"

"Do you think they have some of that yummy chicken and egg stuff Kelly made for me?"

What? My picky familiar was in a five star hotel suite and he wanted food like the kind a *wolf* had made for him? Oh boy.

"I can ask. Anything else?"

"Can I have some cream? I promise I will use the toilet." He batted his eyes at me and smiled.

Thank the Goddess Sterling was toilet trained. I'm not a big fan of litter boxes and neither is he. He hates walking in his own mess and it makes it easier for the both of us when we're out together. He will go outside if he has to, but never in front of strangers. He hates it when people make a fuss about his bathroom preferences. So, you can imagine my surprise when he used the facilities at Tooth & Nail. In fact, all of us were pretty shocked.

"Sure. Whatever you want, Buddy."

I called room service and the snippy waiter named Jay told me they would try to make something pleasing for Sterling, but I didn't hold my breath. After all, according to Jay, "The hotel wasn't accustomed to creating gourmet special dishes for animals." Whatever. Since when was a plate of scrambled eggs and chicken breast gourmet? I listened as he rattled on, repeating his long spiel.

"Like I said, we don't do this very often. Especially for animals. But since you are in the Honeymoon Suite, we'll make an exception. Your food will be there in about thirty minutes." The snooty waiter hung up before I could even utter a "Thank you".

"They say they will try to do it this time, Sterling. But as for breakfast, we're on our own. I'm sure they know who I am and it's another act of snobbery. I've been thinking we should move when all of this is over. I don't know how much more snootiness and horrible treatment from these people I can handle."

"The townspeople will stop once the Council clears you of the charges."

"I doubt it. These people have changed. I've changed. It doesn't feel like the same Salem Ridge anymore."

I flopped down on the bed and turned on the TV. Nothing interesting was on, so I lay there staring at the ceiling. Next thing I knew, someone was knocking on the door. I knew it couldn't be our food so soon, so I prepared for another demonic attack. But would a demon knock? Who knew what the crazy fuckers I'd been dealing with were capable of?

"Just a sec."

The maitre'd wheeled our food cart in and I handed him a huge tip.

"That was fast. Thank you."

He turned on his heel and left without saying a word.

"I hope they didn't spit in our food."

"Yuck. Was that necessary, Mistress?"

"Sorry." I snickered. "I forget how sensitive your stomach can be."

I removed the cover from Sterling's dish and placed it on the table. When I picked up the cover to mine, I found a note taped to the underside of the lid.

"Enjoy your meal, Cupcake. See you soon." There was even a devilish smiley face at the end.

"**Ugh!**" I threw the lid down and took Sterling's plate from him.

"Hey!"

"We can't eat it, Sterling. Shawn sent a note with our meal. He might've poisoned it."

"Do you really think he'd poison our food? They need you alive, remember?"

"I'm not taking any chances."

"Now, what will we eat? I'm *starving*." He collapsed on the bed with as much kitty drama as he could muster, even feigning a momentary lapse of consciousness.

I rolled my eyes and said, "I don't know. Jeez! All I wanted was a shower and some rest, I can't even have that! This five-hundred dollar oasis of a room is turning into such a waste! Why did I think I'd get a damn break?"

When I threw myself onto the bed, he pounced onto the enormous pile of pillows and lay down beside me. "Mistress, it will be okay." His whiskers touched my cheek and he rubbed his chin against mine.

"You keep saying that. I'm just not sure I believe it."

"I've got an idea. Let's call Keith! I'm sure he will bring us some food and then we won't have to be alone. He can sit here with us while we wait for the Council's enforcers to show up. Plus, it might cheer you up having that big, strapping puppy-eyed man around." He smiled and purred. I swore he winked at me.

Suddenly, Mr. Snooty-Pants wanted to play matchmaker and who was I to argue with his sudden approval of Keith? "Sure, why not?"

Kelly answered the phone at Tooth & Nail and said she'd send Keith over with a care package soon. Before hanging up, she asked me to give Sterling a kiss for her.

"Seriously?" This was getting to be downright creepy and I shook my head in disbelief as I hung up the phone.

I laid a big ole kiss on top of his head. "From Kelly." He acted all offended but he didn't wipe it off. If I didn't know better, I'd say my cat had a crush on a dog. I knew him too well and he had it bad for Kelly.

"I can hear you again, Selena. And no, I do not have a crush on Kelly. We are nothing more than very good friends."

"Right, overnight, you and Kelly, two mortal enemies, have become bosom buddies? Friends, you and a dog? Ha!"

"She's not a dog, she's a wolf."

"Ohhh. She's a wolf now is she? My mistake." I laughed as I opened the sliding door to the balcony and breathed in the scent of spring blowing across the river.

"What's the big deal?" Sterling followed me to the doorway. "You wanted us to get along, didn't you? After all, we will be family soon." If his grin were any wider, his face would've split in two.

"What?"

"Keith is your soul-mate. Stop denying it. You love him and he loves you. Besides, it's predestined, there's no stopping it. The book said so. That's why Samell wanted you to be kept away from Keith."

"What? Why? I must've missed that page."

"Keith comes from a long line of demon hunters. That's what his mother and brothers were hunting the night they were killed. It was an ambush."

"Oh."

"Yep, Samell sent Shawn and Roberta to kill all of them. They were all supposed to be there at the cabin for a family bonding trip while getting rid of a few demons. Kyle, their father, was stuck behind and running late because the beer delivery guy showed up with the wrong order. So, he called Katharine and told her he would bring Kelly and Keith up later with him. Around ten p.m., Kyle had set out to drive up there when the phone call came in. Another pack leader had stumbled upon the carnage and immediately cleared his pack out of the forest."

"Oh my Goddess, what a horrible thing to do!" My own supposed father had murdered everyone I cared about. When would it stop?

"Kyle sent Keith away and kept Kelly at his side. Raising two changing wolves and running the business by himself was too much to handle right after the murders. He feared they would be picked off one by one. Keeping Keith safely located in Tennessee, ensured there would be a male to step up as pack leader if Samell killed Kyle, and Kelly was a wreck. For weeks she stayed inside crying after her mother and brothers died."

"So Samell sent Shawn and Roberta to kill them because of me? Why?"

"Your powers and revenge are why. Add in the fact that your mom and Katherine were friends and you've got yourself a pretty close group of demon hunters, allies. Katherine and Elena held Samell prisoner until the Council arrived to imprison him in his own Hell."

"It's making more sense now. But why keep Keith and me apart?"

"Because Mistress, if you mate with Keith, you will be the biggest threat to demon-kind ever. You'd both be unstoppable. Plus, your demon blood gives you insight into how demons think and behave. Your witch blood has the answers on how to subdue them and send them to Hell. If you mate with Keith, you will be able to not only foresee their actions, stop them and send the demonic puke-faces back where they belong, but you will also be able to *kill* them. You're a triple threat waiting to happen."

"Me? You've got to be kidding! Why would Samell create me if he knew I was going to become so powerful? Seems kind of stupid if you ask me."

"He only saw what you could do *for* him. He had no idea you were predestined to be Keith's mate. He was not privy to the knowledge of the book. You need to stop doubting yourself, Selena. You might feel like a scared little girl, but inside you're one helluva danger to demons. If you mate with Keith, you'll be one wicked bitch!"

"You've been dying to say that, haven't you?"

"Maybe."

"So, all in all I simply have to mate with a wolf and save the world? No pressure there."

Another knock at the door announced the arrival of my alleged soul-mate and ended the conversation with Sterling. I opened the door and everything in my world was right. When I looked at his smiling face, my insides turned to jelly and ignited a fire deep in my core. Every fiber of my being yearned to be held in his arms, to feel his heartbeat against mine and my body silently begged for his. The mere twelve inches we stood from each other was too far. My destiny was right there in front of me and I hoped I would be able to live long enough to embrace it

"Hey, Kitten."

Why did that one word turn me to mush? I'd never been a fan of nicknames, but everything the man said caressed me like soft hands that rubbed my worries away. His sexy, southern drawl alone was an aphrodisiac, combined with his charming personality and well-built body inherited from great genes and hard work, it was enough to whet more than my appetite.

"Hey, yourself." I blushed and held the door open wider for him to enter.

"Come on in."

"Fancy digs." He whistled.

"Yeah, it's alright, I guess."

"Hey, Buddy. How are ya?" He rubbed the top of Sterling's head after putting our sacks of dinner on the table.

"Hi, Bro!"

Bro? Were they going to give each other high-fives, too? It was so weird watching these two creatures who were supposed to be enemies act like besties, but it was also nice in a Twilight Zone kind of way. I figured I should just stop questioning all of it and enjoy the good stuff.

"I brought your favorites."

The aroma from our favorite food joint had my stomach gurgling and pleading for sustenance. Sterling clapped and giggled like a silly school-girl before he realized Keith's watchful eyes were on him, clearly amused. Sterling cleared his throat and sauntered across the floor, playing the 'cool cat' card instead.

"That should be fine," he said as he launched upwards and strutted across the mahogany table with an air of indifference.

"For you," he turned to me, "I brought a turkey club, fries, salad, and sodas. I also have more out in my truck. You can stock up your mini-fridge *or* maybe you'll decide you'd rather come home with me? You already know I cook a mean breakfast." He winked and turned on that panty-soaking, crooked smile.

Did he practice that in a mirror? Damn, the man was tying me in knots and we had barely said ten words so far. He was absolutely perfect. Everything about him screamed 'pure temptation'. Well, except for the whole 'changing into a dog' thing. But I could get used to that, I supposed.

Don't get me wrong, I love animals. But the idea of kissing Keith, knowing he could—and probably did—lick his own ass and balls was just a bit stomach-turning. Not that it should be different if I were to...*um*...give him a blow job and then kiss *him*, but he's a dog right? And I wouldn't suck him if he was in dog form. So...

"Selena!"

"What? Holy balls you scared the shit out of me! Why are you yelling at me, Sterling?"

"Because I've been trying to get your attention for a few minutes, but you were in la-la land."

"Oh. Well, excuse me." I rolled my eyes.

"Next time, you might want to filter your thoughts. Some of us don't need the visuals." He glared at me and flipped his long, gray tail.

My eyes darted to Keith who stood there grinning at me and he raised one eyebrow.

Shit! I forgot they *both* could read my thoughts! I turned an incredible shade of crimson as heat filled my cheeks and glanced away quickly. "Let's eat," I mumbled.

"Yeah, I'm suddenly very hungry, too," Keith said.

How I was able to blush any more than I already had, amazed me. But there I was, red, hot and bothered all over again.

* * * *

After we ate and discarded our containers, Keith and I walked out onto the balcony while Sterling bathed himself again. We sat there watching the river barges float down the Ohio River. Their decks were loaded with coal and from a distance, the sunset cast shadows, making the piles look like mini-mountains. "If only I could move mountains like that."

"You can, Selena. You have to believe in yourself."

"How, Keith? I've never had to fight anything on my own before this week. In the past three days I have had more action than I've seen in my entire life."

"See? And you made it through that." When he squeezed my hand, it sent electricity through my entire body. The closer we became, the more I felt pulled to him. We were like magnets. I leaned in to kiss him and as soon as our lips touched, I craved more. His tongue slid into my mouth, searching, teasing, and he tasted sweet like his tea. Keith wrapped his hands in my hair, pulling me closer. My own hands explored his arms, his chest, as my pulse quickened to a steady, rapid staccato. Then without warning, he broke our kiss.

Breathless, he held my face in his hands. "My entire life, I've wanted to kiss you, to love you. I never believed I'd have the chance. I figured you'd be with that asshole, Richardson, forever."

"So why are you stopping? Shut up and kiss me some more." I smiled and tugged on his shirt, pulling him up against my body.

He held me in his arms and sighed. "Because, Selena, we still have some talking to do. There's more you need to know, more to learn before we just go jumping into bed together. If I don't say these things now, it may be too late. Once I start loving you, I won't want to stop."

Gulp. Deflated, I sighed in defeat. My raging hormones would have to wait. Though I appreciated his gentleman-like attitude, I had needs and if they weren't fulfilled soon, I knew I'd blow a gasket. "Okay, let's talk."

"You might be mad at me for a few of the things I'm going to say, but you need to understand that I don't intend to hurt you."

"Keith, really, let's just talk. Let me decide if I will be mad or not. Okay?" The sooner we finished talking, the sooner I could get laid.

He told me he had seen Shawn with not only Roberta, but with many other women from town including Janice. He knew Roberta and Shawn were demons, but their strong financial ties to the town could've put the community in unnecessary hardship if Keith had made a move too soon. Though Keith felt I should've known all along about Shawn's deceit, he also believed I would've thought Keith was nothing more than a meddling gossiper and jealous loud-mouth.

After he told his entire side of the story, he added "I'm so sorry, Selena. I never should've stayed silent. Hurting you is the last thing I would ever want to do. But I won't tell you that I'm sorry Richardson and you are through."

I sat down on one of the Adirondack chairs and listened to the river as its waves gently lapped at the rocks below us. I was too exhausted to be angry with Keith, besides from what Kelly had said yesterday, I'd already gathered he'd known about Shawn and Roberta all along. However, I never would've imagined Shawn and Janice. Then again, I was way behind in Shawn's tally of conquests and frankly, I was sick of hearing about Shawn.

I knew Keith was being honest and he'd done what he thought was best, not only for me but for his father and the entire town. This was more than I had done for any of them recently. My thoughts swirled around in my mind and I chose my words with care, before speaking.

"I know you could listen to my thoughts if you wanted, so I won't try to say it doesn't upset me."

"I wasn't invading your mind this time, I promise. I'm a bit scared of what you're thinking, so I'm controlling myself."

"First, let me say you should have told me. You should have let me decide if I would've believed you or not. You didn't trust me enough to let me make up my own mind." I turned to face him, my eyes full of compassion. "But you were right. I wouldn't have believed you. I thought I was in love. I believed in so many things that have turned out to be so very wrong. So, I don't blame you. How could you have known what I would do or say?"

"For the record, I've always wanted you to kiss me. When you left, I was hurt. I couldn't be there for you when your family was killed and I was alone when mine was. It sucked. I blamed the craft, I blamed the goddesses and I blamed everyone except for the demon I fell for. And that really sucks. I've been an idiot for so long. But I'm glad you're back and I'm glad you kissed me, even if it ended too soon."

"*You* kissed *me*." He teased.

I smiled and said, "Are we okay now? Can we get back to that amazing kissing and maybe move on to other more amazing things?"

The smile on his face disappeared. "Not yet. I mean, we're okay. But there's more you need to know."

"There's more? Like what?"

"The prophecy about us."

"Oh. Okay, tell me."

"It was decided before we were even born."

"Sterling filled me in on most of it."

"How does he know anything about it?"

"He overheard Kelly and you talking last night. He told me just a little while ago."

"Did he also tell you about the mating?"

"Yep."

"So, you're okay with me biting you?"

Biting? "No one said a word about *biting!*"

"Well, that's the only way to make you mine, Selena."

"Marriage and sex don't work for wolves?"

"No. I mean we *can* and will get married, if you want. But to be one of us, you have to be bitten, marked."

Holy balls! I felt so very ill.

"It's not like I bite a chunk out of you. In fact, I've heard it's quite pleasing to the receiver. At least until you go through the change. But that's another conversation we will have later."

"Change? I have to, um, change?"

"Yeah, change."

"What will I change into? I'm already a mix of craziness! When will the 'change' happen?"

"It can occur anywhere between twelve and seventy-two hours after you're bitten. Kelly, Dad and I will take care of you. Dad should be back soon and believe me, there's nothing to worry about, Kitten. You'll be safe and well taken care of."

Nothing to worry about? He wanted to chew on me like some meaty-bone and I shouldn't worry? Oh, and then I get to become a wolf? *A bunny murdering, squirrel-eating wolf!* Right, not a thing I should be concerned about there.

"I know it sounds scary, but it's your destiny. How about I just leave for a bit while you think it over and you can call me when you're ready to talk some more, okay? But know this Selena, I love you and I won't let anything happen to you. Even if we haven't mated, you're already mine." He stood to leave.

Sterling's words from earlier mixed with Keith's and I knew they were both right. But I still had questions and I was so nervous!

"Keith? What if Samell finds out we've mated and he tries to kill me? How will I stop his little demonic party if I'm dead?"

"He won't know."

"Shawn showed up here earlier and said he could smell you on me. They've been watching me. I know it's because of this damn ring. It won't come off!"

"I won't let them kill you, Kitten. I promise."

I knew he was telling the truth. I could feel the honesty and integrity rolling off of him in waves. With him, I'd always be safe. Keith was a family man and more intelligent than I'd ever given him credit for. He must know what he was doing. Maybe it was the only way to defeat the parasites that were gunning for me?

Deep in thought, I must've looked lost. Keith wrapped his arms around me and kissed me on the top of my head. I knew with complete clarity what I had to do.

"Bite me."

Chapter Thirteen

"What?" he stepped back as if I'd smacked him.

I pulled the collar of my shirt to the side, "Bite me."

"Selena, maybe we should slow…"

"Here, I'm ready. Just try not to hit my jugular, okay? I'm kinda' fond of living and blood is a bitch to get out of fabric. Besides, if I bleed out, I can't zap the mess away, if you make one. And…"

He began to laugh, a full-on belly laugh. Why was he laughing at me? Embarrassed, my hackles rose and I crossed my arms over my middle.

"What's so funny, Keith? That's what you wanted, wasn't it? Here I am giving you permission to snack on me and you're laughing at me."

"Aw, Kitten. This is why I love you." He closed the distance between us, his eyes tender and full of love as he said, "Every day and every night I want to make you smile and laugh just like you make me smile and laugh."

I walked back into the room and Keith followed.

"I'm glad I am sooo amusing. Yeah, folks I'm here all week for your entertainment. Don't forget to tip your waitresses," I mumbled and flopped myself down on the bed.

"Please don't be mad. I didn't mean to laugh at you. You're just so damn cute!" He tucked his hands into his jeans pockets and walked over to me.

"Selena?"

I refused to look at him.

"Kitten?"

"I'm not your…"

"Yes you are. Look at me."

"No. Besides, I can't be a kitten if you bite me. I'll be a dog, a wolf. 'Kitten' doesn't make any sense."

"Stop pouting or I might have to spank you, Kitten."

My jaw dropped and my head snapped up. "You wouldn't! I swear you're trying to push my buttons, Keith Jacobs! As if I'd let you spank me like I'm some naughty child! You wouldn't dare!"

He turned on that tempting crooked smile and I could feel heat settle in my middle, battling with my injured pride. "Try me," he drawled.

"Keith, you will *not* spank me. Try it and I will kick your ass!"

"Wanna bet?"

"I mean it!"

In a flash, he had picked me up and bent me over his knees. Crack!

"Hey!"

Another crack across my backside!

"Listen here! If you think I will bow to your dominating..." Crack! "Keith, I will not be treated like a child! Let me..." Crack!

With each tap of his hand, the sting was beginning to excite me. I realized his smacks weren't painful and I enjoyed each tap more than I ever thought I would. I knew my ass would show a red branding from his hand and it was turning me on.

"Ready to be good?"

I said nothing. Crack!

"You're a bully!" I giggled.

Crack!

I wanted more so I pretended to struggle and wiggle. Every time he smacked my ass, my pussy clenched with need. My panties were soaked and the rough fabric was creating a glorious friction against my hardening clit each time I moved.

"Silent treatment?"

Crack!

"Kitten?"

'*Don't stop, please don't stop*' my mind begged. My nipples were hard little peaks and desire rolled through me in waves.

Whack!

I was so lost in ecstasy that I didn't realize I'd whimpered, wiggled and ground my pelvis against his thighs with abandon.

"Oh. You like that? I guess I should stop." He rubbed my ass where only moments ago, he'd slapped it. The heat from his hand was soothing the sting and turning me on even more. The contrast from pain to pleasure sent my hormones into overdrive.

"*Mmmm…*"

As I lay facedown across his lap, his hand traced the seam of my jeans from my ass to my clit. Shivers rippled through me as he cupped, rubbed and stroked my covered mound. I could feel his erection poking me through his jeans as he sat beneath me and I hungered for more.

"Selena? Are you ready to listen?"

I shook my head.

He stood me up and I straddled his lap, facing him. "I don't want to listen, Keith and I'm tired of talking. "Grinding my crotch against him, a small moan escaped my lips. "Do you really want to talk right now?" I trailed kisses up one side of his neck, nibbling an earlobe. He said nothing and I pressed my breasts against him and scraped my nails across his back.

He wrapped his hands in my hair, pulling my body down hard to meet his. I ran my hands over his shoulders and grabbed fistfuls of his long hair. I needed to touch him, every inch of him. I pulled his shirt over his head and reveled in the sight of his broad chest and muscular arms. Apparently, being a wolf is very good for the body.

Thank you Goddess! The man was seriously built. Not like those wrestlers on television, all bulgy and covered in veins and hard steroid-induced muscles. Goddess, he was perfect! Firm, muscular and tan with abs unlike any I'd ever seen. For being a wolf man, he wasn't as furry as I'd expected and I was a bit surprised. In fact there was a thin line of dark hair down his middle that trailed into his well-worn jeans. Damn those jeans! They blocked my view of the rest of Keith's goodies. Beneath those cursed jeans, Keith's manhood taunted me like a present that begged to be opened.

When our eyes met, I could feel the heat rising between us. There was an unspoken understanding, like the kind I'd only ever seen in movies or read about in books. We moved, thought, existed as one. So in tune with each other, we sensed the other's desires and needs. This man felt like the other half I'd always searched for. His touch filled me with an inner peace I had never known and my spirit cried with relief with every kiss we shared.

He stood up, cradling my ass with his hands and held me against him. Though held in his hard-working hands made me feel dainty and cherished, my body ached to be ravished. Every touch, every look, filled me with longing. My heart was full, but I needed him inside of me. I couldn't get close enough to him and his masculine scent drove me into an absolute frenzy of desire.

Sensing my urgency or perhaps due to his own dwindling control, he stood me on my feet and gently raised my arms above my head. He pulled my shirt up and off of me as if the cotton t-shirt was made of the finest silk. How he could be so methodical was a mystery to me. All I wanted was to rip all of our clothes off, practicality be damned! His eyes never left mine as I unbuttoned my jeans. Grabbing my belt loops, he pulled my pants down my thighs with ease and they puddled at my feet along with all of my worries.

"Selena…"

"Shh, no talking."

Keith took off his jeans and briefs, tossing them to the side before I could tear them off of him myself. His cock was standing at full attention and I felt another wave of ecstasy roll through me along with a thankful prayer for the large present he had for me. I shimmied out of my bra and panties just before he wrapped his arms around me again.

As his length pressed against my mound, his lips left a trail of hot kisses across my shoulders. I knew he was holding back and being gentle, but I needed more. I needed to release the primal lust inside of me before I exploded. I nibbled his bottom lip and pushed him towards the bed with my body.

"Not so fast, Kitten." He spun me around and tossed me onto the heavenly mound of down and silk before joining me on the bed.

Keith slid his hands up my legs, leaving a trail of heat in their wake. I squirmed under his touch, craving more.

"You're so beautiful, Selena."

His lips caressed the inside of my thigh as his fingers rubbed my clit. I arched my back, raising my hips off the bed. He placed a hand on my stomach which set off another wave of heat from just that one touch as he held me in place.

Passion and desire rolled through my body and my senses came alive. His every touch spun my senses out of control. Wave after wave of white hot heat poured through me and when he moved his hand away in search of more skin, I whimpered from the chill left behind and begged him for more.

His mouth covered my soaked pussy and he slid his tongue into my core. I wrapped my hands in his hair moaning as he devoured me as a starving man would ravish a ripened plum. I lifted my hips, rubbing myself against his face as his licks intensified.

He pinched my clit with one hand as his other slid up to squeeze my breast. The blood rushed back as he released the hard little nub, creating a pain that turned to such sweetness, I thought I was losing my mind. My first orgasm slammed into me with explosive fury and I screamed his name as he lapped at my cream.

My eyes rolled back into my head as I writhed in ecstasy and begged him for more. "Please, Keith! Now!"

He climbed up rubbed the head of his shaft up and down my pussy, coating himself in my juices. Positioning himself above me, he shoved the tip of himself inside. I grabbed him by the ass, trying to shove him in deeper and he pulled away slightly. Over and over, he barely dipped inside me until I was out of my mind with need.

As I moaned and begged, he plunged himself into me, filled and stretched me with his cock. He pounded into me and I lifted my hips to match his rhythm. I found his weak spot when I pinched his nipples and he let out a primal growl as he neared the edge of oblivion.

"Here we go, Kitten. Ready?"

"*Mmhm…*"

He lowered his mouth to my breast and I wrapped my legs around him, taking his full length as far into me as it could go. As we both rocketed towards climax, he bit my already tender breast and I screamed in euphoria. I felt my eyes change and I couldn't breathe, but I didn't care. *More, more!* My body and mind screamed, begged in unison for everything he had to offer. His hot seed poured into me and my muscles milked him for every last drop. Swirls of colors danced before my eyes and I heard him say, "I love you, Kitten," before the darkness claimed me and I slid into unconsciousness.

* * * *

I was surrounded by a warm cocoon and everything felt different. I was safe, protected. I snuggled down into the comforting silk and my face rubbed up against something hard and solid, shocking me awake.

"You're still here? I thought I was dreaming."

"Where would I go?" Keith kissed the top of my head and rubbed my arm.

"What happened?"

"You passed out, again. But don't worry, I've heard that it happens alot."

"How long was I out?"

"Only a few moments. You okay?"

"Never better." I looked down to where he had bitten me and I could see it was already healing. "I should hop up and get in the shower, but I don't want to move from this spot. Ever."

"Don't worry. I've already cleaned you up, Kitten."

"Really? Thank you. You didn't have to do that." No one had ever done that for me before. The man was incredible! I didn't know whether to feel embarrassed or cherished. All of it was such a new experience and I had no idea how to behave.

"Yep. All nice and fresh again. I promised to take care of you."

I swatted at him playfully. "Then let's get messy again."

"I will enjoy hearing you say that for the rest of our lives, Kitten."

"After I change, won't it be weird calling me 'Kitten'?"

"You'll always be *my* kitten."

"You still haven't explained why you call me that."

"Okay, don't laugh. You've always reminded me of a kitten. You're soft and sweet, needing someone to guide you and take care of you. But like a cat, you don't want anyone to know that. You pretend to be invincible and strong, daring to test the limits without concern about consequences, always getting up even if you fall down over and over again. You're full of energy, love and surprises and I know you'll always keep me on my toes. Selena, I know how I've described it isn't perfect, but you're everything I've always wanted and I can't stand the thought of you not being in my life."

Keith held me tight as I traced lazy circles on his chest with my finger. He was right, his words weren't romance novel perfect by any means, but I'd never been a fan of cookie-cutter romance books. They always seemed too good to be true. What Keith had said meant more to me than anything some author could've written for their make-believe characters. To me, his speech was beyond perfect and lying beside him in that moment I was as content as a kitten in a patch of sunshine. Maybe the name fit after all.

"When I...you know...is it going to hurt?"

He waited, taking a moment before answering. "Honey, I honestly don't know. Probably. When I went through it, yes, it hurt like hell the first dozen or so times. But it got easier. And you can always practice."

"Practice? Like every full moon, practice?"

"No, not just during a full moon." He laughed. "Anytime. You can change whenever you want after you get the hang of it. When you're ready, I'll show you."

"You will?"

He kissed the top of my head, "Yes, but I can't explain what will happen or how it will happen. You are unique."

"Is that because I'm a half-breed?"

"You're not a half-breed, Selena. There are many reasons this will be different. But yes, the fact that you are half-demon, half-witch does change a few things. It's been unheard of until now. So, there's no guide book for this."

"Great. I'm the first? I'm going to be an even bigger freak." Rolling over, I tossed the sheet aside and stood up.

"Kitten, you'll never be a freak. I don't ever want to hear you talk about yourself that way again. Understand? You are unique, special and I love everything about you. Please, don't worry so much. I promise I won't leave your side."

I tried to give him my most convincing smile before I walked into the bathroom. The rat's nest that had taken the place of my long, blonde hair needed serious attention and of course, after making love, my bladder screamed to be relieved.

"When you get back, you can tell me about those bruises on your beautiful body, Selena."

Shit! I'd forgotten about the fight with Shawn. Keith was going to flip out!

I finished my business, washed and dried my hands. The long, sometimes painful process of brushing my 'just been fucked' hair began and as I stared into the mirror, a violet-colored mist appear behind me. Armed with a hairbrush, I turned around slowly, speechless, as I watched the most gorgeous woman I'd ever seen, materialized right before my eyes.

Though she was beautiful with her waist-length, raven colored hair and eyes the color of spring violets, my mind screamed 'Demon!' She had to be another friend of Roberta's. No one could be as goddess-like as she was without it being a trap. Maybe she was one of those sirens, women who lured men to their deaths below the murky surface of the sea. But how on earth would a mermaid get in here? Oh yeah, bathroom, duh.

"What do you want?"

She spread her arms wide and the bracelets she wore linked to a necklace made of the most beautiful alexandrite I had ever seen, shimmered and shined as she moved, casting prisms of color all around the room. And I noticed she didn't have fins or gills. I surmised she wasn't a mermaid and my mind ran through the various 'pretty' demons I'd read about, but she didn't match any of the pictures I could recall.

"It's time, Selena."

"Time for what and who are *you*?"

"My name is Amaris. I'm an enforcer for the Council of Elders."

Right. This beautiful woman with a voice that flowed over my body like satin was an enforcer? Please! More like lust demon. Every word she said tickled and touched me, pleasuring me from across the room. I hadn't even remembered I was naked until my nipples stood out in tiny painful peaks.

"*You're an enforcer?* All goddess-like and standing in my hotel bathroom? This place must be a beacon for paranormal activity," I said as I looked around the room, ready to whip some ass in case anyone else decided to join our impromptu party.

"What do you mean, Selena? I was sent to get you and here I am. There's no need for modesty," she said matter-of-factly as I grabbed a pink, fluffy robe and slid it on, my sarcasm lost on her.

"Well, I'd feel more comfortable if at least one of us wasn't naked, Amaris. No offense." The woman would be a perfect muse for any artist. She was flawless!

"You need to say your goodbyes. It's time to go."

"Can't I have a little more time? Keith and I…"

"I'm well aware of your recent activities. But I was sent here to bring you back with me and we are on a tight schedule. I will allow you a few moments to inform your familiar and your wolf friend but then we must leave."

I knew I was supposed to be a strong, fierce and self-assured witch, but my lip trembled and my heart felt like it was breaking. Keith and I had finally found each other and I'd just been bitten! Who would take care of me when I went all fangy and fuzzy? What if the Elders thought I had rabies and tried to put me down like some common street-mongrel? Oh my Goddess!

"My familiar, Keith and his sister planned on being witnesses for me at the trial. And I can't just…"

"There is no need for witnesses," she said harshly.

Meow! 'Miss naked and full of hotness' was quite temperamental, wasn't she?

"The Elders have everything they need, Selena. They are awaiting your arrival as we speak."

"So, I have to go alone?"

"Did you not gain the Council's attention on your own?"

Though it pained me to admit it, she was right. I had to do this on my own. I blinked back tears and said, "Okay. Just give me a minute and I will be back."

"No. I am to escort you wherever you go."

"Great. Can you at least cover yourself?"

"Why would I do that?"

"Never mind."

Keith was already dressed when we walked into the bedroom suite. Thank the Goddess for small miracles. I would've gone ape-shit crazy if I caught 'Miss Hot-Body' ogling my wolf!

Sterling stood on the bed, his eyes the size of saucers as we approached. "Mistress, what's going on?"

"I have to go."

Keith spun around, I saw his confusion change to understanding and he was embracing me in the blink of an eye.

"Everything will be okay. After we tell them our side, they will understand."

"You can't go. They only want me." Before he could protest I said, "It's fine, Keith. I'm a big girl. Will you please take care of Sterling? The room is paid for so you both can stay here if you want. No sense in it going to waste."

"We'll be right here, waiting for you."

He never even looked at Amaris, further proving he was a keeper. Keith kissed me with unbridled passion and Sterling rubbed against my side.

"Selena, we'll stay right here. You just tell them your side. You can do this!" He stood up on his hind legs and placed his front paws on my chest, looked me in the eyes and said, "Believe in yourself. We believe in you, Mistress."

I rubbed his head and wiped a tear from my eye. Kissing him on the nose, I whispered, "I love you, Buddy."

Tears pooled in his eyes as he whispered for the first time ever, "I love you too, Mistress."

"We need to go, Selena."

"Just a minute!" Keith held onto to me, protecting me as an alpha would, as a true man would.

He planted his lips on mine one more time, once again filling me with more love and hope than I'd ever had my entire life. "See you soon, Kitten. Whatever happens, we'll be right here."

Tears threatened to pour out of me and I nodded my head, afraid to speak, afraid that would be our first and only goodbye.

As the purple mist swirled around and swallowed us, I waved goodbye to my soul-mate and turned to face the next part of my so-called destiny.

Chapter Fourteen

"Amaris, where are we going?"

"Summerland."

Shit. My trial was in Summerland? How could that be? That would mean the Elders were loved ones and friends who had passed on, right?

Summerland is the paranormal's version of the Christian 'Heaven'. It's the realm where souls are judged and where people awaited their next lifetime. Filled with so many different realms and lands, one could never see everything Summerland has to offer. I had no idea what to expect for I had only heard stories and folklore, but I can honestly say I was scared shitless.

The mist around us dissipated as we stepped into the most amazing place I'd ever seen. No wonder most people weren't sad when they died or sad when their family and friends died. From what I could see, Summerland was paradise! We were surrounded by rolling hills and trees of every color, size and shape as we walked across the softest blue-green grass I had ever seen. There were more species of flowers lining the path than mankind could ever name. Each species was brighter and more beautiful than the last.

"It's so beautiful! It's like a mirror image of Salem Ridge, only more vibrant and alive."

"It is the parallel of your world, but untouched by chemicals, pollution and time."

"Are my parents here? Will I see them?"

"I don't know, Selena. My orders are to bring you for your trial. The Elders didn't tell me anything else."

"It's probably for the best anyway."

We walked on and on passing winding creeks and waterfalls where people dressed in bright, flowing clothing talked and laughed. There wasn't one frown or sorrowful gaze. The people enjoyed their afterlife and all that went with it. I wondered if they'd been as happy before they died or if it they'd acquired a bigger sense of peace after they'd passed. No one acted as though they missed their families, friends or former lives. I felt like I had stepped further into the Twilight Zone.

"Is everyone here dead?" I couldn't stop the questions that bubbled up inside and I hoped Amaris wouldn't think badly of me. However, she had to know what I was on trial for. The Elders and residents of Summerland probably discussed me quite often. The failure and idiot I'd been had to have been a hot topic, considering who my parents and other relatives were. My imagination ran wild with images of people lining the streets and stoning me in the town square.

"Some are." Amaris's sudden answer startled me and I paid close attention to every word she spoke. "Others have chosen to give up their powers and ties to your world in order to stay here. And then there are others who are trapped here for many different reasons."

"Trapped? Why would anyone feel trapped here?"

"It is not for me to say. There are many things about this place I don't even know."

"Really?"

"I would not lie to you." Her answers were clipped and concise. Nothing in her eyes betrayed what her feelings were. How could a woman so beautiful have no emotion?

"I believe it," I whispered. And I also believed Amaris had no idea how to smile.

"I smile when I'm not working."

"You can read my mind, too?" Lovely. I swore nothing in my life would ever be private again. Everyone I knew could tap into 'the Selena network' whenever the desire struck them and it began to irk me. Why was it even necessary to speak telepathically? To me, it was nothing more than a huge inconvenience!

"Of course I can read your mind. It's part of my job to read the thoughts of others, Selena and I take it very seriously."

Of course it was. So, in order to keep myself from thinking anything else that might've gotten me into trouble, I continued watching the various people as we walked along. They were all happy. It made me speechless to see such bliss. And I was a bit confused. This place was an enigma!

"There is only happiness in this realm. Other places are much darker. There is a realm for every possible emotion and crime."

"Every emotion?"

"Yes Selena, even one for lust." I saw a small smile creep across her face.

Yes, she smiled! I blushed at the mention of 'lust'. Again she'd read my mind and had probably seen the movie-like playback of memories from my prior round of lovemaking with Keith. I felt like I was surrounded by paranormal peeping-toms! Oh no! If Keith and I were connected telepathically, surely Keith and Kelly were also able to read each other's thoughts! Kelly would know every, sordid detail of my and Keith's sexual escapades, every time we made love! Oh Goddess, the humiliation radiated from me in waves. How would I ever be able to face Kelly again? And then, I thought of Kyle! The embarrassment kept getting worse and I hadn't even been face-to-face with Kelly or Kyle yet.

Amaris and I rounded a corner and came upon an immense clearing. I saw wolves of every size and color frolicking in a field of wild daisies. As we approached, they all stopped playing, trotted over and bowed their heads as we walked by. I returned their gesture and smiled.

"They know and welcome you. Those wolves are the guardians of our realm and no one harboring ill-will may enter. I may be able to read people's minds, but those wolves read people's hearts. Yours is pure," Amaris stated.

"What? How do they know that? How do you know that?" Shocked, my words came out in a stuttering mess and again I felt naïve and inferior. Everyone knew more than I did about the world, more about me than I did. It was very unsettling to realize how sheltered my entire life had been. There was so much I needed to know. How did anyone believe I would be able to defeat demons such as Roberta, Shawn and Samell, let alone save all of the people who depended on me? I was in way over my head and the water just kept rising.

"Our wolves can sense you have been marked. You are now their kin, part of the eternal pack that lives here."

"I haven't even gone through the change yet. How can they possibly know?"

"Can't you see that *anything* is possible here? To them, you are a queen, marked by a next-in-line alpha."

Gulp. "Queen?"

"There are many sides to you that will appeal to many creatures. Your powers, your gifts will be sought by many. Evil, good and in between, creatures will crave everything about you."

She then pointed to a ridge covered in black clouds and shadows. "That's where we are going. Follow me and watch your step. If you fall, there will be no saving you."

My heart dropped. I wanted to stay where it was sunny and the people were happy. I'd never been a fan of cloudy, cold days and that ridge up ahead did not appear very inviting. In fact, if misery were a picture, that ridge is what I would see.

We came to a stone bridge, and I could tell that each rock had been placed by hand. It was perfect. How something so beautiful could exist in this dark and frightful area of Summerland amazed me. Below us, water as clear as glass trickled over stones and created little waves and dips as it babbled along a hundred feet down. Amaris was right, it was a long way to fall. The bridge seemed to go on forever, and with every step I sent up a silent prayer the bridge was as sturdy as it was pretty. I know we crossed it in no time.

A large, gray castle loomed before us. Dark and menacing, it was the complete opposite of everything I had seen so far and very fitting for this particular realm. There was no light source, no sun or moon. The trees, or what used to be trees, were blackened and charred. I didn't see one animal, person or insect out and about. I had the distinct sense that no creature other than a demon could have survived for very long in that realm.

Lightning cracked across the sky and thunder rumbled beneath our feet as we approached the giant building standing in the mist. No, it wasn't because of me. In fact, my powers felt like they were gone. The air was charged with palpable electricity and the very atmosphere seemed to feed on it. This couldn't be where the Elders lived! Who were the people inside? Were they even people? What exactly was inside that place? My nerves were raw but I wasn't about to cry or show weakness, so I straightened my shoulders and followed Amaris.

"Are you sure this is the right place?" I knew it was, but I had to hold on to a tiny, glimmer of hope that she'd messed up, didn't I?

She said nothing and we walked on. A huge wooden door opened of its own accord and my stomach flipped as the forty-foot tall slab of cedar slammed against an inner wall. The only noise that broke through the electrical storm around us was the cavernous echo that ricocheted off of the castle walls.

"Wait, Amaris. I know you work for them but can you tell me how worried I should really be?"

"There are no worries in this realm, Selena. Nothing here can be changed, the outcome is already decided. This is the realm of truth and justice. Here, no fancy lighting or trickery can block the truth and justice is truly blind until the truth breaks through, setting one free. Justice cannot and does not hide in the darkness, it merely uses it as a magnifying glass. Do you understand?" I dared not say no and merely nodded to Amaris while I hoped she believed me.

"Good. On the other side of this castle lie the realms of regret and sorrow, along with many others of the unhappy sort. Those realms torture the body, mind and spirit forever with no relief. If you were going there, then I'd tell you to worry. That's what those realms are for."

"Lovely."

We came upon another wooden door. This one was warded and carved with the many runes that were carved into my book. There was even a matching aquamarine gem in the middle of the door. This one however, was the size of my head. I had no idea what the similarity to my book meant, but somehow it gave me a sense of belonging and strength in light of what had happened so far.

"Here we are, Selena." Amaris laid a hand on my shoulder and it was the only emotion I had seen her express on our journey. "Good luck." Her eyes were kind and full of understanding as she turned to leave.

"Thank you, Amaris. Will I see you again?"

"One never knows." She shrugged her shoulders and I waved as she continued on her way.

Taking a deep breath, I traced the runes with my finger in the same order I had when I opened my family's book and when I touched the enormous jewel in the center, it glowed and the door swung open into the enormous room beyond.

"Come in Selena. We've been waiting for you to arrive. I trust your journey was a good one?"

On either side of me were long wooden benches filled with people who appeared eager for the witch trial to begin. I made my way down the long aisle amid their whispers, pointing and stares as I tried to hold my head high, feigning courage. I came to a stop at the center of the room. At a massive table made of the finest mahogany, adorned with hand-carved symbols and obviously well taken care of, were the three women who would decide my fate. Two of them I had known my entire life and never thought I'd see again. The third was someone I'd never met in person. My mother and Keith's mother sat beside a woman who could be my twin, her resemblance to me was uncanny. I only knew who she was because it was her picture, her story I had read in our family's journal.

My many times removed great-aunt Elizabeth sat in the middle chair. I could tell hers was the highest place of authority here and my mother and Katharine were her co-Elders. It took every ounce of control I had to keep myself from flying across the table and hugging all of them. Though I was supposed to be a great and powerful witch, all I wanted was to hug my mom, to have her tell me everything would be alright.

I saw kindness in each of the women's eyes, but they also portrayed a seriousness that I dared not dismiss. I could feel the many glares of the people who were seated behind me, watching every move I made. I could sense their displeasure with me, their disdain for my past actions and a shiver of fear ran through me as I looked around with the intent of showing strength. It became apparent they were the jury of my so-called 'peers'. By the hateful, disgusted looks on their faces, I knew I was fucked.

"Selena, did you hear me?" My great-aunt asked.

"Yes ma'am. Sorry, I wasn't ignoring you. My journey was fine. Everything is so beautiful here."

"You turned your back on all of this beauty at one point, did you not?"

I hung my head, stuffing my hands deep into the pockets of my fluffy, pink robe. "Yes ma'am. But…"

"Selena, the charges against you are enormous and they've gotten worse," my mother said.

"Worse? How could they be any worse? I know I made some terrible judgment calls but if I had only known…"

"Silence. Your chance to defend yourself will come soon enough. The evidence provided accuses you of murder by magic, using magic for personal gain, using magic for revenge and attempted murder by magic."

I had no choice but to refrain from answering and keeping my mouth shut proved more difficult the longer my great-aunt spoke. There's no way they believed I murdered any of those people! I looked around the room in disbelief, searching for a sign from someone, anyone, that they also believed this trial was preposterous. Nobody would make eye contact with me. They all turned their heads and whispered to their neighbors, but none of them gave me any sign that they were on my side. I was on my own.

"What? You obviously know I did *not* kill my mother and father. And Keith's mother can tell you it wasn't I who killed her or Keith's brothers. She's sitting right there, ask her!" The words flew out of my mouth before I could stop them. There was no one to defend me and I'd be damned before I would go down without a fight. I had too much to fight for and I was not going to be the quiet Selena they wanted me to be. This could be my only chance to stand up for myself and I wouldn't waste it.

Maybe my emotional state wasn't stellar, but I wasn't a murderer. I may have been an idiot, but that was over. I knew what I had to do. Those people needed me, yet all of them acted as though I was some huge inconvenience. I guess I should have been grateful they'd taken the time to stop bathing naked in the waterfalls to come to Castle Grey Hall just to convict me. Silly me!

"Selena, you *will* restrain yourself and speak with respect."

"Sorry. But you cannot expect me to accept that you would believe I've done those things. And attempted murder of whom?"

"We have no idea what to believe. That's why you're here. The attempted murder charge stems from your fiancé's house being blown to bits four hours ago. It reeks of your magic."

"Fiancé? Don't you mean demon? And he is no longer my fiancé! The only thing tying me to him is this damn ring that won't come off! Yes, I have thought about killing the slimy bastard a million times, but I didn't do it. I wasn't anywhere near his place. And I haven't been, for over four months! It wasn't my magic!"

"Really? You burned your own property and home to the ground, did you not?"

"Yes, but…"

"You were also present when your parents and Katherine and her family were killed, were you not?"

"NO!"

"And didn't you call on your powers to fight a woman named Roberta McManus?"

"She is a demon! My half-sister, as a matter of fact, right, Mother? And I didn't start it. She did. It was self-defense. Was I supposed to let her kill Sterling and me?"

"We could also charge you with killing your familiar, Selena."

The crowd in the galley gasped, appalled at my alleged, magical, murderous rampage. "Oh please." I rolled my eyes at them. "Everyone knows I would never kill him on purpose. He means the world to me! It was an accident."

"Didn't you also bind your fiancé in the Honeymoon Suite at the Upton House Inn while you threw lightning and fire balls at him?"

"Again, self-defense!"

"Selena, please?"

"Please what, Mom? Stay silent and get railroaded by these trumped up charges? Let more people lie about me and gossip about what they think they know?"

"*Selena*," my great-aunt Elizabeth said "*I'm warning you.*"

"And I'm warning *you*. I will not be lied to, lied about and stand here like a patsy any longer. I didn't do anything horrible. I did not kill anyone! Yes, I blew up my house. I did fight Roberta and Shawn, but they're demons. A *fact* that I would've been prepared for had my own parents not lied to me my entire life."

My mother's face paled and I felt horrible, but right was right. How dare they sit there condemning me for things they could've helped prevent?

"Yeah, Mother. Keith told me. The answers he didn't have, the book filled in for me."

I knew my eyes were glowing. I could tell by the looks of fear on the faces of everyone in the room. Inside I laughed as they cowered in fear of me. A bunch of pathetic, weak minions were going to decide my fate? Well, I'd give them a show if I had to, if it was the last thing I did.

"Selena, there are other ways to deal with anger. I *suggest* you calm down and listen to me, young lady!" My great-aunt shouted.

The galley erupted in shouts of "Guilty!" and "Lock her up!" People were pissed-off and scared. Without any true evidence they wanted me to hang for crimes I hadn't even committed. Like I'd thought, the whole trial was a bunch of bullshit! It didn't matter what I said or did, they'd already made their decisions and I was screwed.

"Really? Calm down? You have me on trial with bogus evidence, your people are ready to lynch me in the town square and you want me to be the one who calms down? You gotta be fucking kidding me!"

"Take her away!"

"What? You can't! I'm not finished!"

"Guards, now!"

Suddenly, I was frozen where I was standing. No matter how hard I tried to speak, I couldn't even move my lips. My mouth felt like it had been gagged with a thick rope. I could move my eyes and all I saw was fear from the people who surrounded me. I guess I'd gone all freaky again. One woman had passed out and there was a group of ladies trying to revive her. Somehow, this made me giggle. Shit, they hadn't seen anything yet!

"Selena, you will be put into a cell by yourself. We will let you know when we have reached a decision. Until then, I suggest you use this time wisely and do some very deep soul searching."

Decision? How could they make a decision when they hadn't even shown me their 'evidence'? Where was the 'truth' Amaris spoke of? What about the wolves? Great-aunt Elizabeth should ask them about me, they knew I wasn't capable of murder! Everything Amaris had said was bullshit! Just lies to get me to this horrid, dank and filthy castle for a joke of a trial.

Two men in white robes carried me like a sack of potatoes out of the room and down many flights of stairs. They deposited me in a dark, cold cell and I was powerless to stop it. They sat me on the floor after many attempts of trying to prop me up on the stone slab of a bench had failed. One of the men brought me a cup of tea and a tray of food that I couldn't even consume. I guessed they had some sick sense of humor. Hell, they probably would get off on watching me starve while being able to do nothing about it. Like putting a piece of cheese just out of the mouse's reach. Sick bastards!

I was being treated like some common criminal! As I looked around at my meager surroundings, I realized that's what I was. A criminal. I didn't care about my rights until I lost them, until it was too late. I didn't just lose my rights, I lost everything because of my own actions. It was over and as I wept silently, I knew I had no one else to blame. Exhausted and depleted, I fell asleep on the hard, stone floor, alone.

Chapter Fifteen

I assumed it was hours later but I had no way of knowing how long it was before another of those kind, caring and comedic guards showed up to inform me, "They've reached a decision."

Yippee. They were so tight-lipped around that place. All I could discern from him was what my eyes saw. He wore shabby clothing, no shoes and had a beard of gray hair that reached the floor. Other than that, I knew nothing about the man. Maybe it was better that way and maybe that's how the Elders wanted it. No names, no relationships, to keep prisoners wondering and scared.

The man left and I sat there in my robe trying not to think of a bathroom and some underwear. What I wouldn't give for a pair of skivvies and a bra! There was no point in worrying about the 'decision', I knew that. It had been out of my hands long before now. Yes, I was frustrated, but my night of rest had shown me that my desperate outbursts had sealed my fate and I could only ride the ever-swelling tide of consequences or be drowned by it. Never a quitter, I chose to ride it out.

The odds were stacked in the favor of demons. Shawn and Roberta were right, I would be blamed and my powers would be stripped. They'd framed me for that insane list of crimes and gotten away with it. Roberta and Shawn would take everything that meant anything to me and I would be prevented from stopping them. They were going to win. Roberta would have everything she wanted and when these people realized who the real criminals were, it'd be too late.

The next time the doors opened, I saw the Elders had sent five women who I'd never seen before. They placed my hands behind my back but freed my legs and led me through the labyrinth of hallways back to the Council's chamber. Their solemn faces held no sign of what the decision would be, but I didn't need a sign from them. As I walked into the room, I scanned the faces of my peers and realized the decision had been made long before I had arrived in Summerland.

"Selena, I trust you're feeling better now that you've had some rest?"

"Yes, ma'am" I said to Katherine.

"We are well aware of the events that have transpired in the past four years and those that are more recent. We also know the terrible amount of stress you have been under. However, we cannot allow you to run around abusing your powers like you have been."

My mother cut in, her words rapid as if it was her last chance to speak with me. "Selena, I know you have found out the truth about your father. But it doesn't make you evil. I'm so sorry I didn't tell you sooner. Honestly, I doubt it would've helped much if I had. Some things are meant to happen and there's no stopping them. I hope someday you will forgive me and…"

"Selena," Elizabeth spoke again, cutting my mother off. "We are aware that your father, your real father, Samell, has been up to his old tricks again. From the beginning, his plan has been to use you in some way and he has been after your powers since the day you were born."

"I will not help him."

"We cannot take that chance. You are half-demon and that raises the issue of trust. You are not capable of controlling your powers or separating them from your emotional state and that scares us. It also puts us, as well as you, in imminent danger."

I knew that, but hearing her say it didn't make it hurt any less. They were right. Most days, I was a hairpin trigger looking for a gun. Half-demon and half-witch, what could be more wicked than that? Oh yeah, now I was also part werewolf. Goddess, I was a mess!

"However, we also know that you are Keith's soul-mate." I looked at Katherine and she smiled. "My son will guide you through the changes you are about to face. He will show you how to embrace your inner wolf and that will also teach you to control each individual side of you. But we have no idea when your transformation will begin. And for now, we need to deal with your powers and Samell's schemes without counting on you being able to shift."

"Your powers will be bound to your crystal for a probationary period. Whether you choose to help Samell or not, is up to you. He may be able to offer you a way to regain your powers, the choice will be yours. Only you can decide how all of this will end," my mother said.

"I won't do what he asks. He is nothing to me. I don't owe him my allegiance. He created this mess that I've become and maybe he should suffer my wrath."

"Selena, there are no guarantees and you cannot promise something that you may not have any control over. Demons will use every trick in the book and you wouldn't be the first to fall for it," My great-aunt pointedly looked at my mother.

"You don't believe me. I'm not like him, Great-aunt Elizabeth. Sure, by blood he and I are somewhat connected, but that gives me an edge. I see how vile and disgusting demons are. I want nothing to do with them or their plans."

Elizabeth continued on, "The murder charges will be thoroughly investigated and we will rule upon those at a later date if necessary. For now, I need you to show us your crystal."

I pulled it out from under the collar of my robe and held onto it for dear life. Though I'd known all along this could happen, though I had given up on the craft for years, I stood there feeling like shit for having my powers taken from me, like a child who was about to have all of her precious belongings stripped from her grasp because she'd misbehaved. Sure, my powers weren't toys, but I needed them. I refused to cry in front of these people, family or not. I would figure out how to live without my magic, find a way to defeat the demons without them.

I heard my mother's voice in my mind, *I'm so sorry, Selena.* I saw tears in her eyes and I met her gaze with all of the strength I could muster.

Holding my head high and my chin forward, I knew they were taking my powers but at least I hadn't been condemned to that awful dungeon. I vowed I would never again disappoint my mother. Never again did I want to see that look on her face. From now on, I wouldn't let anyone down ever again.

"Do what you must" I said as I let go of the crystal so that it lay against the lapels of my robe.

The three of them, my mother, my great-aunt and my future mother-in-law stood and joined hands in front of me.

My great-aunt spoke loud enough for everyone to hear. "Selena Barnes, daughter of Elena and Samell, you have been found guilty as charged. Your misuse of magic has endangered not only yourself, but all of us. We, the Council of Elders, hereby bind your powers so that you may never harm another living creature. Should you try to regain your powers, you will be brought back here to the dungeons to live out the rest of your days. Do you understand?"

"Yes ma'am. Er, I mean ma'am's."

My mother wiped a tear away with the sleeve of her sky blue dress. She looked so beautiful and I wished we had had more time together. Time that hadn't been spent with me getting my ass handed to me by the Summerland authorities.

Aunt Elizabeth called upon Isis, the goddess of nature and magic. The blessing of Isis was a necessity for any spell cast by a witch. Without such a blessing, a witch ran the risk of unnecessary karmic kick-back. If a witch used magic without permission, the consequences were dire. In essence, Isis was called upon for guidance and help in all matters whenever any witch needed assistance. She was our counselor, friend and confidante. If we said thank you and praised her, she would continue to be there for whatever we needed. I hoped someday I would find myself back in Isis's favor. Until then, I would remain on her list of misfit and problematic children.

A strong wind blew out every candle in the room and papers flew all around us. The people in the galley yelled out and there were a few screams as an unseen force entered the room. There were no windows, no sun or moon, yet the room lit with every color of the rainbow. Swirls of pastel beams shot out of my body, hovered around the ceiling and combined to make the most brilliant green light I had ever seen. The beam of light bounced around as if confused before slamming into my crystal with enough force to drop me to my knees. Chaos continued all around us as I knelt on the floor panting and gasping. It felt like my very soul was being ripped from my body.

"I'm so sorry!" I wept. "I promise I'll never mess up again, please just stop!"

The three Elders raised their arms to the ceiling and in unison shouted, "So it is, so shall it be!"

I collapsed to the floor full of shame and regret as Katherine approached me and said, "Selena, you will be okay. I promise.

This is for the best, dear." She touched my face before walking away.

For the best? I was about to be pounced on by three demons who wanted my crystal like it was demon meth or something and I was powerless to stop them. These Elders had done exactly what those demonic assholes wanted. Now, I would be bait for Roberta, Shawn, Samell and any other demon with a set of balls. Yeah, everything was going to be just damn peachy!

"You will be taken to a room to rest for a bit. Soon, an escort will arrive to take you back to Salem Ridge. I wish we had met under better circumstances, niece. You're a beautiful, strong woman and I wish you the best of luck."

The three of them hugged me and my mother whispered, "I love you, Selena. Trust yourself. The answers are within you. Be safe."

Hugs and words to placate my broken spirit were all I was given. Not the loving and tender family reunion I had envisioned. What a freaking crock! Weary and beyond exhausted, all I wanted was to go home to Salem Ridge. I needed to get as far away from these people as soon as possible, back to my life and back to my real family.

A new young woman came to lead me away by the hand. I was too depleted to make any sarcastic comments about her not needing to restrain me that time. I reached up to hold my crystal for comfort and it felt repulsive. I couldn't stand to touch it and I didn't even want it around my neck. Whatever the binding ceremony had done, had changed it. My lifeline to the universe had been severed and it sickened me.

"You must leave it on," the woman said as I attempted to lift it off of my neck. Her eyes held sympathy and I realized she was also bound. "It isn't so bad, really. You'll get used to it."

I really didn't believe her. She knew nothing about me and I wasn't there to make friends, sympathetic or not. Her words were useless to me. We weren't the same and who did she think she was, telling me I would 'get used to it'? Not me, never. Besides, it wasn't like she had a herd of demonic jerks coming for her or her miniscule abilities. She had no idea what I was going through.

The woman opened yet another wooden door and gestured for me to step inside. "Brightest blessings, Selena. May the Goddess be with you." She shut the door, leaving me before I could come at her with a snarky comment.

"Same to you," I said to the closed door.

I sat down on a lemon-yellow chaise that reminded me of my hunk of junk Beetle that only a few days prior I had smashed into nothingness. The sight of that simple chaise stabbed my already wounded emotional state and I kicked the ugly piece of furniture as hard as I could. That went well since I wasn't wearing any shoes!

"Goddess! I'm an idiot!"

I sat on the floor and rubbed my injured foot as I stared at the rose-colored carpet and walls. I felt so different. Anger and defeat soon diminished and my spirit, though not quite carefree, was a bit lighter somehow and I didn't understand it. With no idea what I would do when the demons came for me, I knew I had no choice except to let things happen as they would. I wasn't in control anymore, if I'd ever had been to begin with.

My mother's parting words came back to me and though she wasn't in the tiny room with me, I questioned aloud, "So the answers are within me, huh Mom? I wish I knew where."

Of course, there was no reply.

Amaris showed up a short time later and we retraced our steps through Summerland. When we arrived back at the entrance, once again we were surrounded by a swirling violet mist and stepped through hand-in-hand. Amaris and I emerged through the other side and into my hotel room at the Upton House Inn.

She waved goodbye, said nothing and retreated back through the mist. I walked through the suite and to my complete surprise there were someone else's things in my room! Frilly pink suitcases with their contents spilled littered the floor and bed. Keith and Sterling were gone! I could hear laughter and sounds of pleasure coming from the bathroom, so I ran out of there as fast as my legs would carry me.

Mr. Fisher was at his post at the front desk and I was slightly out of breath when I reached him. "Mr. Fisher, what day is it?"

"Selena, why are you here? And why are you still wearing that robe? It belongs to Upton House. I demand that you remove it post-haste or I will charge you for it and inform the police you've stolen it."

"Forget about the damn robe for one minute! The day, Mr. Fisher! What day is it?"

"You shouldn't be here, Selena. Your fiancé picked up your cat eleven days ago. Shouldn't you be getting ready for your wedding today?"

"What? Eleven days? I've been gone that long?"

"Yes. You left everything unattended and unpaid for almost two weeks. Do you know how irresponsible you are? I can't believe you're your mother's daughter! Luckily, your soon-to-be-husband was kind enough to pay me and he even added a little extra for dealing with you and your over-sized rodent."

"Watch your mouth! You had no right to allow *that* man to take my cat. Do you have any idea of what you've done? How much damage you've caused?"

"Damage? You dare speak to me of damage? You're lucky I haven't had you arrested. Your cat must've gone insane in that room. Lamps were knocked over, the blankets were torn to shreds and even ripped the paintings off of the walls! That, my dear, is true damage. I'd say you've found an incredible gift by having that man in your life. How many men would pay for the mistakes of your cat or for your complete neglect to uphold your obligations? If you ask me, you've been blessed."

"Mr. Fisher, you have no idea what you're saying. I am far from blessed and I'd appreciate it if you'd keep your condescending attitude to yourself. It's no wonder you're single. No one in their right mind could tolerate your persnickety, nasty personality. If you ask me, you're lucky to even receive customers at this high-priced loony-bin! Maybe I'll bring that up to the Town Council during the next town meeting. I'm sure they'd love to hear how you really behave when no one is looking."

His sneer let me know I'd struck a nerve.

"Can you imagine how they'd feel knowing that their innkeeper was allowing strangers to swoop in and kidnap their pets while they're out sight-seeing? Don't forget how bristly you are to folks who have different beliefs than yours. Remember when you told those foreign exchange students that you couldn't allow them to have their holiday party here? What was the reason you gave? Oh, I believe it had something to do with you not believing in any God or higher power. Am I right?"

"That's none of your concern."

"Really? It may not be any of *my* concern, but I'm sure the Town Council would love to know what a bigot they have running their beloved historic monument."

We exchanged glares across his desk and I refused to break away first. This mutt of a man was not going to intimidate me!

"Now, if you'll excuse me, I need to rescue my cat. After that, I'm coming back here for you, Mr. Fisher, and next time, I won't be quite so cordial. Believe that."

I spun on my heel and I ran out of that inn before he could dial nine-one-one.

Chapter Sixteen

"Keith!"

I burst through the door at Tooth & Nail in a blur of pink and fuzzy, like the hounds of Hell were after me.

"Selena, you're back!"

He dropped the box he'd been carrying, glass shattered and liquid seeped onto the polished hard-wood floor. I threw myself into his arms and he showered me with kisses. "Goddess, I've missed you! Are you okay? Did they take your powers?"

"Yeah, and I'm fine. My crystal glows some weird color instead of the blue I had been taught it would be, but no matter. It's not me I'm worried about."

"You heard?"

"Shawn has Sterling! Wait, where are all of the customers?"

"Selena, they took Sterling *and* Kelly!"

"What? Why?"

"Shawn blew into the hotel room right after you left and he jumped me. He disappeared with Sterling before I could even blink. I'm so sorry, kitten. I gathered your belongings and came back here to find the bar was dark and empty. Kelly was just gone. It didn't take a genius to see Roberta and Shawn had taken her, too. I've had feelers out there trying to find where they've been taken. But so far, no luck."

"Oh, Keith, I'm so sorry."

"I don't know what to do or how to help. Where could they have gone?"

"I know exactly where they are. They're in Hell, Keith. And I'm going to go get them."

"How Selena? Your powers are gone. I'm coming with you. They can't kidnap my family and think I won't kill them for it!"

"It's me they want. Well, me and my crystal. You can't come with me, Keith. I love you more than life itself and I would never forgive myself if you were hurt. Shawn hates you and Samell doesn't want us together. You stay here, stay safe. They took Kelly and Sterling as a guarantee that I would come and deliver the crystal to Samell. They may be rotten bastards but they won't hurt Kelly and Sterling if I bring them my crystal."

After quite a few rounds of him trying to convince me to let him come with me and me trying to get him to understand why he couldn't go, Keith finally conceded.

"Fine. You're probably right, but I'm not happy about it. I know this is your fight. I will be right there if you need me. Just yell, understand me? First things first. You cannot go to Hell dressed like that. I picked up a few things for you to wear. I hope they fit. It's just some yoga pants and stuff you can move easily in. Go try them on and I'll clean this mess up before one of us slips and falls on the glass and whiskey. We'll discuss what we should do when you're finished."

"Thank you for understanding."

I kissed him and tried on the different items he'd purchased for me. He was amazing! Every piece of clothing he'd bought fit me just right. He was the kindest, most thoughtful man I'd ever known and for him to worry about what I would wear when I returned, even though his own sister had been kidnapped, was mind-boggling!

I dressed quicker than I ever had, eager to get back to Keith's side and I enjoyed the fact that I wasn't half naked any longer. I returned to the bar room and planted a big kiss on his cheek.

"You're perfect and I love you." He blushed and shrugged, clearly not accustomed to flattery. To me, that was an even bigger turn-on. He was humble and to be with a man like that was a first for me. Even at such an early stage of our relationship, I couldn't imagine my life without him. With every fiber of my being, I hoped he truly felt the same about me.

After I offered to help clean up the mess on the floor, which he declined because he didn't want me to get cut on any of the glass, we went to the kitchen to scrounge up a quick lunch.

Keith and I washed our hands at the large commercial sink, then he turned to me and asked, "Are you feeling okay? Have you been through any changes yet?"

He walked to the fridge and took out the makings for sandwiches. There was enough food in his arms to feed an army! He must've read my thoughts because he smiled and put back a few items before placing the rest on the large, butcher-block table.

"I'm used to making larger portions for all of the customers we have most days. I guess I forgot it was just you and me." He laughed and said, "So, back to our talk. Anything new?"

"No worries. And by 'anything new' do you mean 'changes' aside from being powerless?" I laughed and shrugged my shoulders when he cast a tender glance my way. "Not that I've noticed. I feel normal. Well, as normal as I've ever felt, I guess. But I also had no idea eleven days had passed while I was gone. Time, everything, is different there. It's hard to explain."

He piled roast beef on a bun slathered with mayo and cut it in half for me before he placed it on a plate with some potato chips.

"Let's finish this conversation out front. You can grab a seat at the bar and I'll join you. If any customers do decide to stop in, I want to be right there."

"Sure, sounds like a great idea."

We walked out front, Keith pulled out a padded barstool for me and I hopped up with ease. He put my sandwich platter in front of me before walking behind the bar, loading a glass with ice and pouring me a soda from the fountain machine.

"Better?"

"Much. Thank you again. You sure know how to take care of a girl." I took a rather big, unladylike bite of my sandwich and moaned with delight. I swear, everything Keith touched was amazing!

Being with Keith was so easy. I didn't feel inferior or stupid. He took care of me without making me feel like a child and I wasn't sure whether I could get used to it. But I knew one thing for certain, I didn't want to mess up our relationship or lose that feeling. I would move Heaven and Hell to keep that man as happy as he made me.

Happiness, true happiness wasn't something I was used to and Shawn had never done anything for me. Okay, he did sometimes, but only when it benefitted himself and I knew his actions were all lies, so everything he'd done for me amounted to nothing in my eyes.

"I missed you, Kitten." Keith leaned in and kissed me softly. His arm wrapped around my back as he sat beside me on another stool. For the moment, I was safe.

"Me, too. I just wish we were all here together."

He cleared his throat, clearly not eager to talk about what we should do. "Do you have a plan? Any idea how to get Kelly and Sterling?"

"Not yet. But I've never been great with plans. I figure I'll just wing it. For now, I just want to enjoy a few moments with you."

I couldn't help myself, I shoved my meal aside and planted kisses all over his face before I hopped onto his lap, almost tipping the stool over.

"I'm so sorry, Keith. This whole ordeal is my fault."

"No it isn't." He held my face in his hands and with a lot more confidence than I felt, he said, "We'll get them back, I promise. Everything will be fine."

Another round of heavy petting ensued. The man could get me hot and bothered with just a look. Being on his lap was a sure-fire way to fuel the fire. As it was, I'd waited eleven days to be back in his arms and I planned on staying there as long as the fates would allow.

* * * *

We were suddenly being applauded as I heard, "How very, very sweet. Look at the puppy love. The whole room is filled with the stench of it. Makes me sick. You both make me sick." Roberta stood behind us, examining her claws before mock-vomiting all over the bar floor.

"You bitch!" I screamed and flew at her. Keith grabbed me by the tail of my shirt, holding me beside him. I knew it took all of his self-control not to rip Roberta to shreds because we both knew we needed her alive to find Kelly and Sterling.

"Selena, no!"

"That's right, Selena. Be a good girl and listen to your master."

"Fuck you, Roberta!" I squirmed and wiggled to get out of Keith's grasp so I could slap that smug smirk off the bitch's face, but he held tight. I was stuck.

"Wolf boy, you better keep your bitch on a leash or her kitty cat will lose another life. He only has five left."

"Ugh! I'll kill you, you fucking demon fuck!"

"Takes one to know one," Roberta sang it like an eight-year-old little girl.

"Real mature, cunt." I hated that child-like voice she resorted to and it irked me to no end when she portrayed herself as an innocent woman instead of the trash-talking-piece-of-shit she really was.

"Roberta," Keith held me by my waist. "What do you want?"

"Why, your bitch's crystal, of course." With dramatic flair, she rubbed her greedy paws together, almost salivating.

"No way, whore."

"You give it to me or you'll never see your fur-ball or his mongrel sister again." She glared at us with her yellow beady eyes and pointed at Keith with one long talon.

"Take me to them," I said.

"Selena, no!" I shrugged away from Keith.

"The only way you're getting my crystal is *after* Kelly and Sterling are released, Roberta. After they are safe, sound and here with Keith I will give it to you."

"Selena!"

"Keith, shut up."

"Yes, Keith shut up." Roberta's sly grin turned her face into a mask of pure evil. "So, let me get this straight. Miss Bitchy-Witch wants to go, no, is demanding to go to Hell and make a deal with the Devil, huh? Offering yourself in trade for a mutt and some ancient pussy? Very noble and honorable, Selena. Stupid, but just what I'd expect from a coward like you. Why fight, when you can surrender, right? Myself, I find your willingness to sacrifice your own life for those creatures rather disgusting and I don't know what Father sees in you."

I bit my tongue until it bled, knowing that whatever I said would only escalate and fuel another argument with the demented whore. "Take me to them now, Roberta."

"I could take your crystal right now and go back and kill them, Selena. I don't need your deal."

"Really? Try it."

She wrapped her hands around my neck and I stared right into her eyes. Her face changed from puffy red to green and scaly, still I showed no fear. No matter how she tried, she could not and did not scare me. Disgust me? Yes. Scare me? Never. I was past being frightened by her insane theatrics. And as soon as I got the chance, I would tear the cunt limb from limb.

Roberta yanked on the crystal, but it wouldn't budge. The chain held and she pulled her hand back, howling in pain. "You bitch! What did you do?"

"Nothing. I don't have any powers, remember? I told you, you couldn't take it. Take me to Samell and free my family. Then, I will hand it over."

Her plan to steal the crystal for herself thwarted, Roberta relented, knowing she had no other choice but to accept my offer. "Fine, let's go."

"Wait! Take us both!"

"Aw, such a good dog. How sweet. Are all of you this sickening? 'Take me! Take us both!'" she mocked. "No! You stay boy, you can wait for the rest of the nasty vermin you call family to return." Roberta patted him on the head as Keith snarled at her. She wiggled her fingers at him, yanking them back but not before Keith snatched her wrist.

"If you touch one hair on any of their heads, if you hurt Sterling one more time, I will personally make it my mission to annihilate every last one of your kind. And when this is over, rest assured I will be coming for you and Richardson. We have unfinished business." Keith's eyes changed to a silver-rimmed shade of amber and his pupils shrank to slits as he growled, squeezing Roberta's arm hard enough to draw blood.

"Keith, please. We'll be fine, I promise." I pulled his hand away from Roberta's bloody arm and kissed him. "I love you. I always have. But you can't help me. I have to do this alone."

"Now, witch! I need to get this fixed before I bleed to death."

"You've been warned, demon." Keith never took his eyes off of Roberta, but they'd shifted back to normal.

"Yeah, yeah Roberta. We wouldn't want you to 'bleed to death'. Bye, Keith."

"Kitten, be careful! I love you."

I followed the nasty troll out the door and had no idea if I'd ever be back again. "Time to meet Daddy," she hissed and then she threw me into a black mist that led straight to Hell.

I landed with such force, that I broke the rock floor. "Thanks for the ride, demon-bitch."

"No prob, *Sis*. Now get the fuck up."

She reached for me and I kicked her. She flew ten feet away and slumped to the floor momentarily. Shit! *Where did that come from?* I had no powers. How did I do that? Roberta looked terrified. She dusted herself off and stood a few feet away from me, just out of kicking distance I surmised, and it made me giggle to see her freaked out.

"Take me to them, *now*."

We walked through a maze of hallways that looked a lot like the hallways in the Council of Elders' castle in Summerland. Only here, I expected to hear the sounds of souls screaming in agony and the smell of burning flesh. But there were none. Instead, I could hear laughter, birds singing and a strange musical melody from somewhere above us.

"I thought you were taking me to Hell? What kind of shit are you up to?"

"This *is* Hell, you idiot. The Trillmor realm, to be precise. It's disgusting and depressing as always."

Everywhere I looked, there was beauty. Persian carpets, lamps that would rival Tiffany & Co.'s and hot-spring pools in every other room that were surrounded by gorgeous flowers I had never seen before.

"Yeah, you've got it rough."

"Shut up and walk, witch."

We climbed staircase after staircase. All were covered in bright colored carpets. Each landing had a painting on the wall and all of them looked expensive. I swore some of them were the ones reported missing ever since World War II, stolen by an infamous German leader. In fact, as we walked by one the rooms, my suspicions were proven right. There, inside a room with a bevy of gorgeous, raven haired women, was *the* man himself. The almost bald man with the worst mustache in history was waiting on the gorgeous women hand and foot. Though disgusting, the irony was not lost on me. The slave driver had become the slave. Poetic justice at its finest. I shivered as Roberta and I moved on.

"Yuck."

When we reached the final floor in this part of the castle, Roberta threw open a door and yanked me inside.

"Wait here."

"Where are they? So help me, Roberta, if you hurt them again, I will…"

She said nothing, laughed and walked out. The door slammed shut behind her so hard I could feel the floor shake beneath my feet.

My surroundings could only be described as wall-to-wall decadence. Plush white carpet lay under chocolate-colored furniture. There were vases of white roses on every available flat-topped table and not one speck of dust anywhere.

"Hell has awesome housekeepers," I mused.

My perusal of the room was interrupted when the door opened and a rather dignified-looking man spoke to me. "Selena, you've finally come home." He walked towards me with his arms wide and I jumped back.

"Get away from me, weirdo!"

"Is that any way to speak to your father? You really should show some respect."

"Yeah, I've heard that a lot lately, but you're not my father. My *father* was killed by your demon spawn and her bitch boy. They blew up my parents' house at your command."

"Yes, well, sometimes these things happen. But there's no reason we can't get to know each other. Let's not argue about semantics and frivolous details. We should be learning about each other, not fighting."

"What?" Was this guy on drugs? It would be a cold day in Hell, before I allowed myself to 'get to know' that silver-tongued piece of shit.

He stood before me wearing jeans and a t-shirt. Samell looked like any other normal fifty-year-old man back in Salem Ridge. Well-built, dark hair and even darker eyes, I could see why my mother had fallen for him. But I knew this was only one of his many forms and I wasn't about to be fooled by his Greek looks and 'come to daddy' attitude.

"Walk with me?"

"Where? Why should I? I'm not going anywhere with you until you agree to take me to Sterling and Kelly."

"You really don't have a choice, do you? You're in a strange land, a strange home. I guess you'll just have to trust me."

As if! But I conceded and we walked back down the many flights of stairs.

"Why did that cunt make me walk all the way up there if we were simply going to turn around, walk back down and head outside?"

"Roberta is such a devious little brat." He laughed. "She loves to play with her food."

"Food?"

"Sorry, wrong word. Forgive me. I meant to say she has a bit of a rambunctious side and loves to play practical jokes on others. Luckily you weren't harmed from this one. Many creatures haven't been so lucky. That girl is a handful!"

Jokes? Rambunctious handful? This guy had to be the most whacked-the-fuck-out person I'd ever met. Wow, he had issues!

"I'm sure," I mumbled. "Now, what do you want? The only reason I agreed to come here was so I could get my friends and go back home. You know that, Samell. Cut the bullshit and take me to them."

"In time, Princess."

"I'm *not* your Princess."

"We'll see. I must say, I do love your spirit, Selena. Very much like my own and it pleases me to see what a feisty young lady you've grown to be."

"I'm nothing like you and your words of fatherly love are meaningless. Get this straight, I am not afraid of you, I care nothing about you and I will never be what you want me to be," I said, as we crossed a lush spacious lawn. My harsh words seemed so out of place in that beautiful realm, but the scenery did not change who I was with. I needed to remember that if I had any hopes of getting my friends and me out of there alive.

His dark eyes twinkled as he smiled at me. "So you know what I am, who I am, and yet here you are showing not one ounce of fear."

"I'm not here for you. I want my familiar and my friend, Kelly. That's all."

"What if I don't want to give them to you? You could always stay here with me and rule this legion as you were meant to. The three of us could be very happy together. Look around, it's paradise."

We stood on a white sand beach littered with seashells and a surreal horizon was our backdrop. The pink, purple, blue and gold sky was flecked with an almost too perfect amount of clouds which seemed close enough to touch. There were gray and pink dolphins that jumped through the air and flipped before they dove back below the clear blue surface of the water. Not far from shore, I saw a sailboat heading west. It was such an odd feeling as I stood there. There was no way to not enjoy the view, yet I was next to one of the most feared demons in history and his presence tainted everything about that moment.

"I will never stay here. If that's your plan, forget it. If it's so perfect here, why do you want to get out of here, Samell?"

"Boredom, simple as that. A demon has to have some variety, you know." He wiggled his eyebrows at me and laughed as his eyes changed to flaming red orbs.

"Why did you create me? I've heard their version. What's yours? Am I some 'end of days' abomination, a tool for revenge against the people of Salem Ridge and Summerland?"

"No. You're my daughter, that's all. Yes, I had hopes you would one day return to rule Trillmor with me. But after I was bound here, I created Roberta and I realized none of that mattered. I have a daughter who will stay by my side and rule the kingdom with me for eternity."

"You're lying."

"Maybe."

"Look, I don't need some touchy-feely, movie-of-the-week moment with the father I never met. I have a real life to get back to. Just set my friends free, I'll give you my crystal and I'll be on my way. You can do whatever you want after that. I want no part of it and I don't want any trouble."

Samell eyed me coolly, without a hint of what he was thinking and relented again. "Fine."

He yelled for Roberta and Shawn with sound that was more of an ear-piercing wail than a shout. When I saw them appear, Roberta had Kelly by the hair, dragging her down the beach and Shawn stomped through the sand with hand one hand wrapped around Sterling's throat.

"Stop it! Let them go, you assholes!"

Samell put out a hand to stop me. "I give the orders here, Selena. With your pious speech and actions today, you gave up the right to command anything of anyone in this realm. This is my house and you will obey me!" The last was said with a roar that left my ears ringing and I covered them a moment too late. I knew that sound would echo through my mind for years.

"Now," he said more calmly, "Leave them be, Roberta. Fun time is over." Samell shook his finger at her as Roberta took a jab and swipe at Kelly's face.

Kelly punched Roberta in the face as soon as Roberta had let go of her hair. Sterling swiped at Shawn's legs with both paws before he leapt into my arms.

"Mistress, you're alive! I'm so happy to see you. I've missed you so much!"

"Now, give us the crystal, Selena." Samell commanded. Roberta hopped and danced beside him with glee.

"After they are free, Samell. Send them home and then you get the necklace and powers."

"He said to hand it over, bitch!" Shawn roared.

"Fuck you! You piece of demon shit!"

"Oh, a mouth to match your attitude, daughter? I must say you're looking more and more like me every minute." He laughed.

"What the fuck ever. Send my friends home, now."

"Give me the crystal. How many times do I have to tell you, you cannot command a thing of anyone here, especially me? Are you that fucking dumb, Selena? Or are you just that fucking naïve? I will tear out your innards to get that stone away from you if I have to."

"Take it from me if you can. Roberta tried and you can see she failed massively. In fact, I can still smell the aroma of her fried, ratty, red-orange hair. You created one miserable failure for a daughter and another who can't stand the sight of you. Great job, Daddy." I laughed in his face.

"Witch!" Roberta launched herself at me and Sterling flew out of my arms as we toppled to the ground. I used my momentum to roll her over, punching her as I sat on top of her flabby stomach. When my hands were as bloody as her swollen, fucked-up face, I stood up, and heaved her by her nasty, matted hair and threw her across the beach.

Just then, I heard a cry of pain as Samell slapped Kelly across the face. Her nose gushed blood everywhere and that's when it happened. An anger unmatched pulsed through me. No one would hurt my friends again! Not even these high and mighty demons.

A guttural roar erupted from me and as I flew through the air, my fingers changed to claws. I tackled Samell and ripped his face into slivers before slicing his neck open from ear to ear. It brought me great pleasure to watch as he choked on his own blood. The scent, however, was not enjoyable, it was putrid. Rivulets of acidic, bile-colored fluid flowed under his head across the white sand beach, tainting it with the smell of death and disease.

I'd killed him! I'd really done it! And as the immature girl inside of me did a happy dance, that was enough of a distraction for another demon to pounce. Shawn grabbed me by the collar and yanked me off Samell and tossed me aside. I sprang back up and a primal howl tore through me as I speared Shawn. A look of pure, unadulterated fear raced over his demonic features right before I smiled and tore his throat out with my teeth. Once the life drained out of him, his ring slipped easily off of my finger and onto the blood-soaked sand. I scooped it up with a claw and shoved it into the gaping hole that had once been his neck.

"Fuck you asshole." I know I said the words, but they sounded strange and I couldn't put my finger on what was different.

Selena? I heard Sterling call me, but he sounded so very far away. I cocked my head to the side, realizing I was hearing him in my head. *Your eyes, Mistress. They're beautiful.*

My eyes? Really? At a time like this, he noticed my freaking eyes? He picked that exact moment to tell me they were beautiful? What the hell was wrong with him?

Roberta popped up like a jack-in-a-box again and it threw me into a flat-out frenzy. I saw she was seated right where I'd thrown her. She pawed at her face to survey the damage I'd inflicted and wailed like a banshee in the distance. Why couldn't that whore take a fucking hint? How many times did I have to kill that cunt before she stayed dead? Was there some rule or trick to it? Regardless, she had pissed me off beyond belief and I was so done with her stupid, troll ass!

I ran across the beach at full speed, reaching her in moments. Roberta was covered in fluid-coated sand and shock registered on her face a split second before I picked her up and plunged my fist through her chest. After I'd ripped out her rib cage, I held it up in front of her and smiled. She took her last breath as I pulled more of her insides out and showed them to her before I tossed her back across the beach. She fell to the ground in a crumpled heap beside her lover and their nasty demon blood mixed, eating away the sand like acid.

"I told you not to touch my friends, bitch." I snarled.

Samell morphed into his demon form and loomed over me at more than eight feet tall and boy, was he pissed! I should've known killing him wouldn't be that easy!

"Stop, Selena!" he roared, and mountains that lined the horizon crumbled to dust.

Unfazed, I looked at Roberta and Shawn as they lay lifeless, in their morbid together forever pose and nothing brought me that much pleasure in a very long time. I knew it wasn't over, but killing those two had made my fucking day! When I turned around, I saw Samell had both Sterling and Kelly by their necks.

"So, you've been marked by the wolf? That's too bad. I had such high hopes for you." Gone was his Daddy-dearest voice, what replaced it was dark and menacing. "Now, give me the crystal or I will kill them both while you watch," he growled.

"Selena, don't!" Kelly gasped. Clearly she couldn't breathe and the lack of oxygen had caused her to go nuts. There was no way I would stand by and watch as Samell killed my friends, my family!

"Don't give it to him, Mistress. He will still kill all of us. He won't let us go. Save yourself!"

Every word they said sounded strange. I could hear their heartbeats and everything was so vivid. If I turned my head to the side, I could hear their shallow breathing from across the beach. My own heartbeat raced and pounded in my ears. A million different scents assaulted my nose and every hair on my body stood on end with unseen electricity.

"*Give. It. To. Me!*" Samell said, squeezing their necks harder. His voice sent shivers down my spine and I saw Sterling's eyes bulge as Samell twisted his neck and applied more pressure. He had them both in a vise-like grip and a moment of panic settled over me. I felt like an animal caught in a trap. I felt defeated.

The answers are inside of you, Selena, I could hear my mother. What the hell? How was that possible? Was I going insane? I spun around, searching for the voice. My eyes watered and my throat grew tight. No one else was there on that beach! I begged the goddesses above to help me, I had no idea what to do!

As I watched the life being sucked out of my friends, a strange calm settled over me and I knew the answer to all of my questions. I didn't need help or guidance from above or the great beyond. Nothing mattered except saving Kelly and Sterling. I knew without question what had to be done.

I yanked the crystal off of my neck and held it in the air, watching as it turned black. Storm clouds gathered and lightning struck all around me. The thunder shook the ground with magnificent glee and Samell's smug, demonic face looked unsure, panicked even.

My crystal emitted a high-pitched noise, worse than any high-frequency feedback I'd ever heard. The stone pulsed with energy and danced inside, casting brilliant strobes of blinding light all around us. I threw it at Samell as hard as I could. I saw my friends crash to the sand the moment I had let go of the crystal. Samell was so intent on gaining those powers, he wasn't concerned with Kelly and Sterling.

I no longer cared what happened to the power-yielding bauble and I rushed to my friends on the shore. Above the crashing waves and storm, I heard Samell mutter words in a strange voice. In his hands, he held the crystal, the power he craved, the power he'd desired for years, the power he'd created me to obtain and a giant wind lifted him into the air as he chanted and mumbled. Samell hovered high above us over the sand. I shielded Kelly and Sterling with my body as best I could as Samell rattled on and on in his own demonic language.

The waves grew and swirled under his feet before they crashed back into the huge ocean. Wind tore the clothing from his body and lightning destroyed each piece as it fell away from him. Serpents and reptiles poured out of his flesh and his eyes, full of fear and confusion met mine. I held onto my friends for dear life.

He screamed, "Selena!" just before he vanished in a deafening explosion of flames.

That was the last thing I heard. At that exact moment, everything disappeared and I do mean everything. There was no light. No sound. I floated on a sea of blackness, alone.

Epilogue

After the explosion, I wasn't able to remember much of what had happened. Kelly's throat had taken quite a beating and she lost her voice but Sterling was kind enough to tell everyone every detail. According to his story and Kelly's emphatic nods, I had partially shifted. A brand new thing no one had ever experienced and therefore, yet another quirk unique to me. Then, in the words of my beloved cat, I "kicked some serious demon ass!" No one has heard from Shawn, Roberta or Samell so I'd guess it's safe to say we won.

When I woke up after all Hell broke loose, literally, my mother was holding my hand. Great-aunt Elizabeth and Katherine were smiling ear-to-ear.

"Welcome back, Kitten." And of course, Keith was right by my side.

"What happened? Are we all dead? Did I kill us all?"

"No, sweetheart," Mom said. "You saved us."

"But how? I gave him the crystal."

"Yes, but it had your demon powers in it. When Samell released them, he was devoured by your magic. Your powers surpassed his!" My great-aunt said.

"My demon powers?"

"Yes, dear. You've had your magic this entire time. We never took that away. Just in case you needed some help. We knew you'd do the right thing."

Tears flowed down my face as I stared at them in disbelief.

"So, I'm no longer a demon? Or half-demon?"

"Technically, yes. But, you no longer have demon powers and abilities as you did before. Your blood however, is still mixed with Samell's. Being bitten by Keith has helped dilute it some, though and you will still be able to keep tabs on other demons when the need arises. Call it 'demon radar' if you wish."

"Great."

"I know it isn't what you wanted to hear, Selena. But according to Kelly and Sterling, you are one wicked bitch!" Everyone erupted in laughter at Mother's outburst. Of course, she blushed at her use of such a profane word but laughed right along with us. I knew they'd all been dying to say something about me being wicked and who better than my mother to do just that?

Great-aunt Elizabeth and Mom shared more of Summerland's knowledge with me and I soaked up every bit of everything they said. I finally understood how important all of this was and that was up to me to keep everyone safe, both here in Summerland and back at home in Salem Ridge. My step-father, Joseph, also in attendance, told me how proud he was of me and said he knew I would come around. Apparently, I'm just like my mother.

Kelly and Sterling were inseparable. The entire time Sterling had been in my life, I'd never seen him so attached to anyone other than me. Once in a while, I felt a pang of jealousy, but it was so nice to see him happy.

"If I didn't know better, I'd say he's in love."

"He is, dear." My mother was at my side.

We'd watched Kelly and Sterling walk about the grounds of Summerland, day after day. Often, they would go off together and no one would hear from them for hours. At first, I attributed their relationship to the events of the prior week. But after we saw the looks and glances they'd give each other, it became more apparent their relationship was real. I wasn't sure how I felt about that. After all, Sterling was my best friend and he was a cat. How could a cat and a wolf be life-mates?

"Selena, there are so many things you need to learn. And I know I should've taken the time to teach you the truth about familiars. There's no easy way to say this, so I'll just say it. Sterling isn't just a cat, he's a man."

"What? You can't be serious. I've shared the last twenty-five years with a man? Undressed, gone to the bathroom and done an incredible number of private things in front of a man? I think I'm gonna be sick."

She shook her head and grasped my hand. "Dear Selena, it isn't like that. Sterling was serving his own sentence. Before you were born, he used his magic to cast a spell on a young lady back

In Salem Ridge. Her name was Margaret Wilson, the daughter of a prominent family, a human family.

"He loved her more than anything," she continued, "even more than his powers and freedom. However, his spell went wrong and the girl suffered a nervous breakdown. You know as well as I do, love spells, if cast on the unwilling, can backfire. She became obsessed with Sterling to the point he could not even go to the store without her flying into some fit of jealousy. Sadly, one night while Sterling was in town playing cards with friends, she committed suicide.

The Council, of course, knew of the spell, but at the time they weren't concerned. They felt the spell would die out and never dreamt such a tragedy would occur. Sterling was so distraught he threw himself on the mercy of the Council and surrendered his powers, his life and freedom. He begged them to punish him. Sterling threatened to kill himself, to die and be with the woman he believed he had pushed to suicide. The Council felt he was a danger to himself and others, and he was."

"Oh my Goddess! Poor Sterling!" It was so hard to imagine my wonderful feline friend suffering like that.

"They deliberated for weeks while Sterling was locked in a cell in the dungeons. He refused to eat or drink and he didn't speak one word the entire time. The only company he had while incarcerated was a tiny mouse. He cared for that little rodent as if it was his own child. That one act of compassion proved to the Council Sterling wasn't truly ready to die. It made their decision, though difficult because they all cared about and sympathized with Sterling's plight, a much simpler one." My mother paused, her eyes full of tears. Her heart has always been huge and any hurt another suffered, she felt just as intensely as the person who felt pain, whether it was physical or emotional. Yeah, she's an empath, but I always teased her by playfully calling her a sap.

"He was brought before a jury of his peers, much like you were, and the Elders sentenced him to a life spent as a familiar until the time they saw fit."

Tears rolled down my cheeks, my heart felt like it broke for my friend. He was so much more than I ever knew.

"Now, the Elders, myself included, have been discussing this matter. Yes, he was sentenced to a lifetime without magic. He was allowed to be around it, but it would be impossible for him to practice the craft. Even if he tried, it would not work."

"I can't imagine how difficult it has been for him all of these years! And to be around me when I surrendered my powers and turned my back on the craft! I could have done all of the things he couldn't and I took it all for granted. He must have hated me for that. But he never showed it." Somehow, my heart swelled with even more love for my familiar. "So, he has to stay in cat form forever?"

"Well, we've decided his sentence should be ended. The Elders who sentenced him have since moved on to new lives and we believe he has paid for his actions long enough. His actions since his sentence have been honorable and heroic. To us, he should have his life back. What do you think, Selena? Could you handle not having a familiar? You don't necessarily need one any longer. You have Keith now."

I pondered what my mother said. The thought of living without my best friend felt like it ripped my heart in two. Sterling had been with me my entire life. How was I going to go on without him? But who was I to keep him trapped?

"Have you asked Sterling how he feels?"

"Not yet," my mother replied. "I wanted to speak with you first. It's your call. After all, he belongs to you."

I looked across the garden and saw Kelly and Sterling lying in the grass together. Kelly's arm reached out and she rubbed him under the chin, while she murmured words of love.

"She loves him, Mom. Kelly wishes he was a real man, she thinks he is perfect. Does she know the truth about him?"

"Only if he told her, Selena. But I doubt he has."

"What would you do?" I looked into my mother's eyes and she smiled.

"This isn't about me, darling. This is your choice. Like I said, all of the answers you will ever need are inside of you. You just have to ask the right questions and listen with your whole heart. Whether you like the reply or not isn't important. The answer will always be just what you need to hear." She knew it was not an easy decision and she hugged me as hard as she could.

She was right. I knew what needed to be done. Sterling should have a life, a real life. With Kelly, he could share what was left of his years on Earth and he could experience love, true love. Who was I to stand in the way of that?

"So when should we tell him?" I smiled and I knew in an instant it was the right thing to do.

"Whenever you want, sweetie. By the looks of it, I'd say the sooner the better. Those two need to get started on their life together."

* * * *

A few days after Sterling became human again and properly told Kelly his feelings we had a double wedding ceremony in Summerland, surrounded by our friends and family from both the great beyond and Salem Ridge. It was nice to be accepted by everyone again. Well, almost everyone. Janice was missing in action. No one had seen her for over a week and that was just fine with me.

Kelly and I both wore bridal gowns designed by Amaris. No, they weren't see-through. She'd created a long, white, billowy, silk dress with a halter style neck-line that was perfect for Kelly. I'd never seen her look so beautiful. She literally beamed with happiness and love. My dress was shorter, knee-length, strapless and white, of course. The beautiful garment was made of hand-sewn vintage lace from my mother's wedding gown. To be honest, it was the most gorgeous dress I'd ever seen. No, it wasn't the seven-thousand dollar gown created by Janice, but it was worth so much more. Priceless is the best way to describe how I felt about it.

Sterling and Keith were more laid-back with their attire. Cowboy boots, perfectly cut jeans, button down shirts and hats completed their look. They were the most handsome men we'd ever seen. Keith with his piercing eyes and rugged physique, Sterling with his dark gray, almost charcoal colored hair and his athletic, lean build, both were absolutely dashing. Sterling, of course fidgeted with the collar of his shirt a lot, but he'd never been one for collars anyways. Kelly and I laughed, grateful that some things never changed.

Great-aunt Elizabeth presided over the ceremony, while my step-father and Kelly's father, Kyle, walked us down the aisle. Not one of the pearls or beads fell off of our dresses, none of the lace ripped and neither of us stumbled, so I'd say our wedding went off without any karmic hitches. The only tears that fell the entire day were tears of happiness.

After we cut our wedding cake, Keith pulled me to the side and we left the many guests to enjoy the party. "Ready for your first full moon, Kitten? It can get kind of wild."

"Oh, you bet I am, wolf-man. The wilder, the better. Just try to keep up with me."

"Are you sassin' me?"

"If I am?"

"You wicked little witch."

He playfully spanked me and with no worries, no hint of trouble, off we ran, so I could be thoroughly ravished by my wolf for the rest of our lives.

THE END

About the Author

Madison Sevier is an avid reader and lover of all things romantic. She lives with her amazing husband and daughter, both of whom have shown her how wonderful and magical life can be. Madison spends her days as a homeschool mom and her nights are spent building fictional lives for readers to find inspiration and hope for their own happily ever after to come true.

Other Books by Madison

Natural Lust
Anything You Want (River Jewel Resort 1)

Secret Cravings Publishing
www.secretcravingspublishing.com

33890363R00103

Made in the USA
Lexington, KY
15 July 2014